UNRESOLVED SCARY

STORY

VIVEK KUMAR PANDEY

Contents

Foreword

Author biography in English :MY NAME IS VIVEK KUMAR PANDEY . I WAS BORN IN 30 SEP 2002,I AM FROM SURAT GUJARAT INDIA.MY DREAM WAS TO BE GOOD WRITERS ,MY FAMILY SUPPORTED ME TO SUCCESSFUL AND I CAN DO IT MY SELF.How do I write? That is a question, I believe, that can be honestly answered by me."CELEBRATING YOUNGEST WRITER AWARD WINNER IN GUJARAT 1ST RANK" MR PANDEY JI . I may think I did a good job writing something. The reader is the one who decides the quality of my writing. I do find writing to be natural to me and therefore find it to be a real challenge. My trick as a challenged writer is to do the best I can and know that I am happy with the final outcome. It may take a while to do my best and there may be quite a few problems I run into along the way.

I am not a greedy person those who are thinking about me and my self I never tried it anyone people suffering from sadness ,I trying to get promoted people suffering from happiness and joy in your Life Time. Now in current situation in India and also world people are unemployed and have no many but our indian governor help to people to get free food from ration card , i also take part in leadership team ,i am Motivational speaker , Film script writer. There was my two dream firstly writer and secondly actor & also my own film is upcoming soon i done almost completely completed script for my film .I AM GOING TO SAY WORD OF HEART TOUCH OUT PLEASE READ IT" , firstly i thanks my father he supports me in this field they always getting inspired me by own his words and behavior ,they always said that he was a biggest person in the world in future and also they purchase fruit and chocolate for me in anytime & anyway , firstly my father buy him then call me Vivek you want a chocolate i will say yes papa but how many tell me ,papa: you tell me how much i buy him i told 1 or 2 chocolate but my father purchase whole the boxes of chocolate and they get suprised me. MY FATHER WAS BORN IN " 20 SEPTEMBER" 1971 IN INDIA.

1) MY FATHER FAVORITE CLOTHES IS KURTA PAIJMA AND ALSO STYLES SHOE

2) FAVORITE SINGER IS KISHORE DA

3) FAVORITE STATE GUJARAT AND KOLKATA , HIS VILLAGE IN BIHAR

4) FAVORITE COLOR BLACK AND WHITE

THEY ALSO LOVE cricket like IPL and one day t-20 .they also like watching a News daily and heard the song daily ,they also interested in tik tok video but in current time tik tok is banned in india but also few videos are in you tube. In lockdown time my family and me very enjoy day daily. my father play daily ludo with his sister and son, daughter.they always loved tea and coffee anytime call me "। . I make it tea for my father but some reason after the April to june they are suffering from fever and cough , weakness on 6 June 2020 my father death. they not told me say bye bye his life. After death of 6 June on 10 june my mom and dad anniversary.but my father is Best in the world they can do anything for me please take care of father and respect it of your parents.

CHAPTER ONE

Dance & Dance

There was a girl who had an illness and was bed-ridden for the majority of her life. She was recently diagnosed to die within the next couple of months so her parents decided to spend as much time with her as they could before her time came. They decided that the best thing was to go camping at a local site for a little bit since the daughter was stuck in the hospital for so long.

On their way there, the girl was quiet as usual and laid in the back while the parents talked amongst themselves. When they finally reached their destination, they pitched the tent, unpacked everything and started a campfire. The mother was constantly filming the area and her daughter while the father went out for more firewood. It was getting dark when he came back, but he suddenly heard the mother scream so he rushed over to discover that his daughter was standing on her feet and was doing a wild, erratic 'dance' before she suddenly dropped dead.

After all the funeral processions and grieving subsided, the parents wanted to see the video the mother recorded on that very night. They put the tape in the player and began to watch. At first it just showed the mother looking at the scenery and random animals that passed by in the distance, but as the time frame skipped, it jumped to when she was inside the tent with the daughter as she stood up and began to jerk around.. But there was something wrong. It first was in the corner of their eyes but as they replayed the scene, their horror became more and more real.

The entire time the daughter was 'dancing', there was a ghastly white hand latched onto the top of her head.

CHAPTER TWO

The Argument

You're the manager for a small store. You hired one of your friends, and you just found out that he's been stealing from the register, stealing stock, abandoning his post to visit with his girlfriend in the back room while he's the only one on duty, and the argument you had with him at the office just didn't settle it for you. You pound on his door. When he opens up, he goes pale, soils himself, and staggers back, gasping for breath.

It doesn't impress you, really; you figure he just thinks you're showing up with the cops, until you step through his door and glance to the side, where you get a good look at yourself in the mirror.

Or at least, the parts of you that are still recognizable after that shotgun blast that your friend gave you at the end of that argument...

CHAPTER THREE

The Smileyman

It was a normal Friday night in Glasgow, Scotland. Clubs were clearly visible, the bright lights and the blaring noise dominating the night.

But with light, there was also darkness. There was one, almost abandoned, housing estate where nothing was there and everything was silent, almost as if a bubble had been wrapped around the derelict housing block. No one went there because it was so dark and eerie. Even during the day, a permanent grey cloud seemed to hang over it. Even the birds didn't sing.

But tonight, someone was going there. A 12-year old boy called Jack, who had snuck out at 11 o'clock at night to go to this place with his friend, 13-year old Paddy.

The two boys climbed the rusted fence. Paddy had a flashlight, but due to low battery it was very dim. They followed the bush clearing to the housing estate, and it was pitch black. They emerged from the clearing to see a long row of blocky houses. In the eerie silence they walked towards an alleyway in between two of the houses. The flashlight wasn't going to last much longer, and then they would have to entrust only the dim glow of a half moon to guide them. They went into the alleyway, Jack first. They found a dumpster, and looked at the ground to see a red substance had stained the ground, leaving a trail which led to behind the dumpster.

Jack checked it out, and immediately gasped with shock.

"AAARRGGGHH!!!"

Paddy, taken by surprise, ran out of they alleyway.

"Its a dead body, oh my god, what do we do?" Jack screamed, barely squeezing the words out through his state of sheer panic.Sure enough, a dead body lay there. Headless, it lay there. It had been eviscerated, disemboweled, mangled and cut up in every possible way.

Jack looked towards Paddy, expecting some form of reaction. But Paddy wasn't listening. He was already too concentrated in what was behind Jack.

"WATCH OUT!!!"

The knife cut into the side of Jack's neck, and blood poured out, not the geyser that you see in the movies, but a steady pour down his neck, onto his shirt. Jack fell to the ground, motionless.

Paddy shone his dim light on the creature that had just killed his best friend. It had a black hooded shirt on, with long sleeves. On the shirt it had an upside down Illuminati pyramid symbol printed on it. Also printed were the words:

"Run, fight, but theres nothing you can do. You can be sure though, that Smiley is coming for you!".

The creature also wore a pair of black jeans. But the most distinct feature, for certain, was it's face. Blood red, as if someone had ripped the skin from it's face, and slightly glowing blue eyes. The creature's mouth was also fixed in a permanent yellow closed smile, which stretched almost up to it's eyes.

But Paddy could only see it for a few seconds, and then his light completely ran out, shrouding the alley in complete darkness. His best friend's body was dragged further in, and was swallowed by the darkness. Paddy covered his ears as the creature let out and ear-piercing fit of hysterical laughing.

Paddy dared to take a few steps into the darkness.And then the creature took him.With blinding speed, the creature rushed towards him, and stabbed Paddy in the neck, and held him up like a piece of meat. Paddy took one last gaze into the creature's eyes. The creature once again laughed hysterically, but this time Paddy couldn't cover his ears, and blood began draining from his ears as they succumbed to the pressure, and Paddy slowly and painfully succumbed all together.

The Smileyman had claimed it's next victims. But they surely wouldn't be the last.

CHAPTER FOUR

Death

Light blinds my eyes after what seemed to be a century of darkness. I stood on an unfamiliar highway. I had no idea where I was or how I got there, but I was there now. A man stood in front of me, dressed in a collared shirt and khaki shorts. He seemed to be in his early twenties.

"Where am I?" I asked the man, trying to call back memories of what I was doing before the darkness. The man looked at me, his expression serious, but with a light smile.

"Doesn't matter, my friend. All that does is that you're here. I think you'll find that your memories will return soon. Happens to most people when they die."

"So...I'm dead?" I asked, unable to hide the fear and sadness in my voice. The man jumped, as if surprised by the conclusion that I had drawn.

"No! Oh God no! That would really mess up the plan, now wouldn't it? I'm sorry about the vagueness, but I would rather explain things after you're up to speed."

"Up to speed? What are you talking abou-" I felt my mind seem to bend and suddenly I remembered. The bridge. The dog that jumped out of the window of the car in front of me. The guardrail breaking as my minivan swerved to avoid the dog, sending me falling into the waters below. The water filling my lungs as I struggled to get out of the car. Then the darkness.

"Wait, what happened after I...well, died?" I asked the man, confused.

"Well, let's say you were one of the chosen few. You see, when someone dies and is brought back via resuscitation or whatever other ways Man has to restore life, There is a sort of system. It's all planned. Men have taken to painting a portrait of Death, you know, the hooded skeletal creature with the big sharp scythe. Think of it more like a force. There is no way to control it, and what it chooses happens. One way or another. There is no reason, no cause. But it must happen."

"Why are you telling me this? And who are you anyway?"

"Who I am, is of no meaning. You are the one that matters here. But if it will calm your nerves, my name was Dennis. Why I am telling you these things, you will find out soon."

I looked around at the rather busy highway. Several cars sped past where we stood on the side of the road, not paying us any attention whatsoever. I looked far down the road and saw a large truck coming. A long trailer was hitched to the back, filled with what seemed to be thin metal pipes. About five cars ahead of the truck, a pickup truck passed me, throwing out a bottle of beer as it went. The bottle shattered as it hit the blacktop, leaving jagged glass strewn on the road.

It was too late to pick it up, but most of the cars seemed to see it and swerved around it. The truck came, and although it attempted to pass the bottle's remains, the wheels on the right side of the vehicle spun over the glass, popping one tire at least. The truck swerved, and the driver slammed on the brakes. The gate of the trailer must have not been secured correctly, for it fell open and several pipes fell out at a rather high speed.

I looked on in horror as a car behind the truck attempted to stop, but by then it was too late. The car slowed to a sickening stop exactly in front of me as I looked at the terrible fate of the poor driver. One of the fallen pipes had crashed through his windshield, impaling him. I stared in horror for some time, not sure how to react. I rushed to the man, but I knew there was nothing I could do.

He began to choke on his own blood as it trickled slowly down his chin. The window was down, so I reached into the car to see if I could at least unfasten his seatbelt. It was impossible, and upon realizing this, I stopped trying and pulled my arm out of the car. I brushed his face along the way, and he fell back, dead. A voice behind me startled me from my horrific trance.

It wasn't that of the strange man that I had talked to, so I spun around in surprise. I found myself looking at the man that had just perished before me. He looked from me to the corpse in the driver's seat, and then back to me. I understood. I was Death. The dead man tried to say something, but was overcome with surprise and emotion. Finally, he managed to stutter out a single word.

"W-why?" he asked, trembling all over. Not knowing at all what to say, I thought back to what the man had told me about death earlier.

"It's your time. There are no exceptions. Good luck."

Dennis came from behind him. He put a hand on the man's shoulder, smiling sadly to him.

"Time to go," he said in a voice that somehow immediately soothed the man, who then disappeared as if turned into vapor. Dennis turned to me.

"It's always easier to give the full explanation after the first soul has been passed on. You are now Death, but not forever. You see, there aren't as many cases where someone is brought back to life as there are deaths, obviously. So right now, you are in a hospital bed, kind of in limbo between life and death. And for the next day or so, you will be Death until a conclusion has been made. You were made for this. This was meant for you."

"But it doesn't make sense, if I just watched all this happen in two minutes, how much time has passed for my body where I lay?"

"That doesn't matter. Although I serve Death by departing souls from Earth, I do not know whether Death is an actual person. But regardless, Death has a system that never fails. If you hadn't gotten into an accident yesterday and had been home watching the news, you probably would have seen this accident. Death uses a sort of...well, rip in time to allow a new person to work as Death. It's all so confusing; it's easier to just continue on. So what do you say? Can we just move on?"

"To the next person for me to kill? No thanks!"

"Remember what I said earlier? It will happen. One way, or another."

"Fine."

Suddenly we were standing in a small convenience store. I looked around, wondering who could possibly die. A young man stood by the register, and I hoped that it wouldn't be him. The door opened and the bell jingled lightly. A man walked in with a ski mask covering his face.

Oh God, please no, I thought to myself. The man quickly approached the counter and pulled a small revolver out of the jacket he was wearing. He pointed it at the man, and gestured to the cash register. A woman in the store noticed and suddenly let out a scream. The thief turned to the woman, pointing the weapon at her. The rest happened very quickly.

Three shots rang out, and the would-be robber fell to the ground. The cashier stood with a small pistol smoking in his hands. An open draw behind the counter revealed several rounds of ammunition. I looked down at the dying man, let him bleed for a moment, and then put two fingers on his forehead. I turned around to see another form of the man, without the ski mask. He asked the same question as the first one had.

"Why?"

"Because you're stupid. This is how you spent the rest of your life. Giving a woman a heart attack and making that kid live knowing that he killed someone. Nice life, jackass."

Dennis touched him and the robber vanished.

"Way to be nice and understanding," he said as we went to the next death scene.

We were in a hospital room. Simple enough, lots of people died in the hospital. There were voices drifting into the room from the hall.

"You may want to say your goodbyes. I'm very sorry. It has spread too far into his brain. There is no chance. Once again, I am very sorry." At this, the sound of a woman's muffled cries loudly filled the room. I looked to see a young boy in bed, his hair gone and his face sickly pale. I looked at Dennis.

"Are you serious?" I asked him. "He's got to be less than twelve years old!"

"Remember, no exceptions," Dennis said calmly. I started to approach the boy when there was a knock on the door. I turned to look, and the woman, apparently more composed, entered the room. She walked straight past me and sat in a chair next to the boy's bed.

"Hi sweetheart!" she said, taking the boy's hand into hers. He croaked back a hello, hardly able to open his eyes.

"Now, I know that this is all going hard, but everything is going to be just-"

"I heard what the doctor said, Mom. I love you."

"Screw this," I said to Dennis. "I'm not doing it."

"Fine," he said. "But remember, I warned you."

We were suddenly in the hallway of the hospital, standing near an older doctor and the woman outside the room we were just in.

"I can't explain it," the doctor said. "It's like the cancer just disappeared."

The mother rushed into the room, followed by the doctor. Dennis and I followed. The same boy sat on his bed, completely different. His face had color, and he seemed happy.

"It's some kind of," the doctor began but then suddenly grew quiet. "Do you hear that sound?"

I listened, and I heard it. It was the sound of bacon on a pan. Or, more accurately, the sound of gas escaping a container. Suddenly, the cord to the television that was currently playing fell halfway out of its socket, and a few sparks flew into the air. This was apparently enough to cause a huge explosion, and causing me to have to take the lives of several people.

Including the boy.

"Only one more left to go." Dennis said cheerily.

"And then I get to go home, right? I'm tired of this."

I was so excited to start living again. After about two days of taking over others' lives, it would feel great to actually take a hold of my life again. We were suddenly in another hospital, which happened quite often. In my excitement, I wasn't even paying attention.

"Clear!" a doctor shouted from a crowd of white coated assistants. A bare male chest lifted up along with the sound of electrical buzzing. I approached the crowd and tried to get through to see my newest victim. I looked down at the table that the person was lying on. To my astonishment, and horror, I looked down to see my own body lying on the table. I looked up for Dennis, but he was gone. I'm not sure how long I stood with the other doctors who were trying to save me. But I finally made a decision based on what I had learned. I placed a hand on my corpse, and I was then thrown back into that deep, dark, never-ending darkness that surrounds Death.

CHAPTER FIVE

The Man Who Lives Above You

The man who lives above you is the quiet type. How lucky you are to live in an apartment underneath someone so courteous! It seems he never drops anything, seeing as how you never hear any loud thumps coming from the rooms above yours. He is even kind enough to keep the volume on his radio and TV too low to disrupt you. Come to think of it, had you not seen and spoken to him, you would think no one lived up there. Quite a big change from living below a batch of rowdy teens.

He is terribly kind as well. Within the first week of you living there, he invites you up to dinner and offers his services as a plumber in case you have any leaky faucets. The maintenance crew at this complex is awfully incompetent. You can't have it all, I suppose.

He didn't even get offended when you told him you were far too busy and didn't know him well enough to dine with him. He simply smiled, gave you his number, and let you know the offer stood as long as you lived below him.

One night, you decide to take him up on his offer, seeing as how you're tired of the Hot Pockets your busy schedule allows. You call, uncertain about whether or not he is home due to the utter silence from above, and he answers and invites you to join him upstairs; he has made far too much chicken piccata to eat himself.

You climb the stairs and enter his apartment. It's impeccable. You've already managed to spill some Coke Zero on your carpet. In his six years living there, he has left no stains. Dinner smells delightful. He already has a place set for you, almost as if he was expecting you sooner. Astounded by his kindness, you seat yourself and begin eating.

Almost immediately, you feel a bit drowsy. Overworked, perhaps? He smiles and watches your muscles slowly fail you, the sauce dribbling out of the mouth you can't hold closed. You start to slide from your chair, you can almost feel the floor meeting your body, but no. He catches you. No sound is made. He carries you down the hall, ever so quietly. You're growing too unconscious to worry, so rest assured, no one will hear a thing; you won't even hit the floor.

CHAPTER SIX

Droning

"Hear that?" My brother, Andrew, asked.

"Very funny." I replied.

Andrew looked as if there was something far away, making a captivating noise. Distracting him. He described it as sounding like a police siren, repeating over and over again, barely heard above the cricket chirps of the night and the low humming of the nearby freeway.

"What...is that?"

"I don't know, but it's late. Let's go to sleep."

I woke up and saw my brother at the window of our room, head cocked to the side, as if listening to something very carefully. He looked confused and almost...sad. We went downstairs to join our parents at breakfast.

My Father moved his lips, "You guys sleep okay last night?"

Both my Brother and Mother replied with a "No."

"Me either, kept hearing the cops outside, must've been a busy night," my Dad said.

"No way," my Bro exclaimed, "I had the same problem!"

"Same here." My Mom added.

I noticed my family looked somewhat distressed.

The day went along as usual, but seemed a little... slower, and gloomy. Whenever I was in the company of a family member, they seemed distracted, disinterested in whatever task they were currently involved in. That night we all sat together, watching television. There was a report on the news about many people complaining of an annoying police siren.

"L.A.P.D. states they are not responsible for this, saying that they are aware of the problem and are investigating with their best efforts. We are urged not to worry, as it doesn't seem to be related to a rise in crime." The reporter explained.

"I guess you guys aren't the only ones." I said.

No one responded.

"It's getting closer, Jr." Andrew told me, later that night, as I played video games. "It's so annoying. It's like... right in your face. I hate it."

"What? That noise? It's all in your head. You're just tired. Let's get some rest." I answered.

"Yeah...yeah okay. Night, Bro." He was staring at the ceiling, wide-eyed, as I drifted to sleep.

The next morning, I didn't see Andrew at the window as I awoke. Instead I saw him sitting at his bed, with his hands over his ears, crying.

"Hey, what's wrong man? You okay? Why are you crying?!"

Between sobbing and tear wiping he managed to tell me to go check on our parents. Confused, I still obeyed and went to downstairs. What I saw devastated me. I almost collapsed.

My father was on the floor in a small pool of blood, centered around his head. Makes sense, considering he had stuck small kitchen knives in both his ears. My mother had used duct tape to surround her entire head in the sticky material. It looked like she used the entire roll, effectively suffocating her. I swear I saw her twitch, making me rush back upstairs, to my bedroom.

"Why? Why did they do that? Hurt themselves. Why?!" I asked, frantically

"It's the noise!", He screamed." It's so close! I can't hear myself think. I can't handle this! Ahh! Make it stop! It won't go away. It killed our parents..." He trailed off and looked directly at me.

The whole room seemed to shake as Andrew pounded his head against the wall as hard as he could. I was so surprised, horrified, and grief stricken to do anything but watch. The fifth slam caused blood to spray on the wall, yet he still went on, hammering the barrier with all his strength. He had managed to form a deep crack in his skull. His deep red blood poured out like juice from a pitcher. He collapsed, his hands still at his ears. It looked almost as if he were about to smile.

I never heard the siren that destroyed my life, and presumably everyone else's. I couldn't. I knew my Brother had envied me that moment when he looked in my eyes.I am deaf. I don't know if this is a blessing, or a horrible, punishing curse.What I did know was that the sound was what made my family want to die, and probably many more people.

I knew I was going to be very lonely and sad.

I knew there was no longer the hum of cars from the nearby freeway.

That's It

One day, there was this girl, let's call her Anna. In her hands, Anna held a handful of all kinds of pills. As she stared at them, she was thinking about all of the pain and suffering she has endured throughout her 17 years of life. She looks up into the mirror, stares at herself, and starts thinking. She has been picked on for as long as she could remember and she couldn't take it anymore.

She wanted to end her own life so she would no longer be bullied. No more life, no more suffering, and she was angry. Why does she have to end her own life to find peace? Why is she effected but they weren't? Sobbing, she looked back down on her hands, staring into the pills once more. She whispers to herself, "That's it."

Anna always minded her own business. She was nerd and was one of those kids who were really into bugs and collecting things that most people didn't care about. She had frizzy hair, thick glasses, acne, you know the type. Everybody knows somebody who's somewhat like that. Anna was pushed, shoved, embarrassed, fooled so many times and even raped. She had 'friends' that would talk to her, but later found out that those same friends were telling her secrets to everyone else. The people that she has trusted have been deceiving her too. She felt as if she had nothing to live for.

So what happened to Anna? She's sitting down on her couch with the same pills she had before. As she pulls off the knife from the throat of one of her bullies, she grabs her notebook and checks off a name. She stares into her notebook and swallows her pills. "That's it."

CHAPTER EIGHT

The Monster Is Coming

Thursday night. Everyone was blissfully asleep. Reports had spread of a serial killer in the area, but he would only strike on Fridays, so there was no need to worry.

The serial killer had been labeled "The Monster" and his M.O. consisted of first sneaking into a house, drugging the victims, and then slowly killing them in their beds. The Monster always left behind a signature, a photograph of him in disguise, resembling a black-hooded figure with a blank mask.

Susan casually walked home from a party. She was dressed in a white suit and had her wavy blond hair in a pony tail. She passed by a lit house and saw a couple sitting on the front porch and enjoying the stars. "They're so innocent," Susan said with a soft voice.

The next night:

"Make sure you lock up tight tonight, Ed," said Diane.

"I locked every door, shut every window, and secured every bolt. We're safe tonight." Ed got in bed and kissed his wife tonight.

A few hours passed, not a sound was made. Ed and Diane were fast asleep. A high pitched scream woke them both up. It was silence as fast as it came.

"What was that?!" Ed asked in fear.

"Ellie! Go check her room!" Diane yelled.

Ed ran out of his room and darted down the hall. Before he could make it to his daughter's room, he froze in his tracks to see a dark figure step out of there. The figure had a pale white faceless mask on and stared at Ed. Ed choked on his own scream and ran away as fast as he could.

He didn't get far until he fell due to a piercing pain in his foot. He looked and saw that in his panic, his bare foot had stepped on a knife that was planted for him. He grabbed the hilt, trying to take the knife out of his foot, ignoting the blood that slowly made a puddle. The Monster casually walked towards him, not making a sound in those rubber boots. The Monster put one hand over Ed's mouth, and Ed slowly felt his vision blur as he drifted into a deep sleep.

Ed woke back up, covered in sweat. He looked around and saw that he was in his bathroom, naked, sitting on the toilet, hands tied together under the bowl, and with a piece of barbed wire deep inside a cut in his stomach. He saw his wife in the bath tub, also naked with her hands tied to the spout. A white string was attached to the hot water knob. Finally there was his daughter in her pajamas, standing on the sink. The white string was tied to a board behind her feet, while th barbed wire made a noose around her neck. It didn't take Ed long to figure it out.

Turning on the hot water would drown and burn Diane, this would trip the string and make Ellie fall off the sink, hanging her with the barbed wire and tearing out Ed's vitals. Ed struggled, trying to get free. However, the Monster returned. In the light, everyone got a good view of the disguise. Black boots, black pants, a black trench coat, a hood, white gloves, and a white mask with two black sockets being the only facial features. They gasped in panic as the Monster observed them. The Monster walked to the tub, making them frantic. Not listening, the Monster sprung the trap...

Walking away from the bathroom, Susan removed her mask. she had a disturbing smile, as if she were talking with an old friend, as if the moment in the bathroom didn't happen. She grabbed any evidence and put it in a bag. "This is what they get for relying on those spare-key hiding fake rocks."

Susan was no beast, no ghost, no demon. Susan was only human. But her eyes, those lovely blue eyes, were the eyes of a complete Monster...

CHAPTER NINE

Love Letter

Hello Darling,

I am writing because I now realize that our relationship is fast approaching its end. While I'd love to believe it could go on forever, I've (reluctantly of course) grown tired of our silly routines. The spark has simply faded, and I can't help but hold myself responsible. From the very first time I peered through your window, I knew that you were special. You were different from the rest, and I still believe that. There is something so interesting, so... desirable about the way you carry yourself. The things you do when you believe you are alone. Watching you is what has kept me here for so very long.

In fact, I remember vividly the first time I watched you sleep. You were so peaceful, yet right when I feared I was wrong about you, that I may grow bored of you so early... A laugh. You surprised me, love. You were never like the rest. There is no way you could've been. That is why I fell in love with you. You intrigued me. Nothing made me happier than to spend time with you, To see you in your natural state. Did you know that people are most themselves when no one else is around?

Yes, things were so magical then. Now I've taken to watching you carry out the same routine over and over. You go to work, buy groceries and that is it. What has happened to you? You were once so full of life, now you're reduced to chores and hiding in bed. I have not heard a single laugh in months. Do you realize how much I miss it? I don't think you could ever understand how much you mean to me. How it pains me to hear you cry like that.

I told myself you would never hurt me. That you could never even try. Unfortunately, dear that is where you began to resemble the others. What a pity. Tell me, do you remember the first time we spoke? That day was meant to be so special. I followed you to work that morning, hardly able to contain myself... The excitement of speaking with you that day was far too great. This was at the height of my love for you, in my eyes you could do no wrong. I meticulously planned our meeting, you would never know that I had followed you, and watched you all of these months.

Although when I gathered my courage to speak with you on the train, I was simply disregarded by you. I doubt that you remember our conversation, or the fact that you attempted to ignore me to begin with. I could wager anything in the world that you could not even recall my name if asked today! The conversation was nothing like I had imagined, you dimly passed my attempts at starting it with short answers. Every part of you seemed to reject me, before you even knew me. That hurt, darling.

When I realized that, I let slip a few things I knew from our time at home. Of course I know about your social life, your quirky habits, and even your favorite drinks. I expected a warmer reaction to say the least, I was the one who went out of my way to see you, wasn't I? I knew I understood you in ways that no one else could! That was when you stopped going out. You seemed to want to close yourself off from the world. As if to take your rejection one step further, your whimsical nature seemed to go missing once you knew about me. Did you want to hide all of yourself away from me, to even take away our time at home?

I didn't mean to startle you, or scare you away... I love you. I can now say that possibly going to speak with you a second time was my own mistake, and for that I apologize. I was foolish to come to your doorstep, even though it felt like such familiar terrain. You have to understand how lost I was. I had let my emotions escalate, soon it was not enough to see you. To watch you. No I needed more of you than that. I needed to interact with you once more!

Having said that, our painfully short conversation, and a door in my face... Well doesn't sit well with me. I would simply love an apology for that. What disappoints me the most is that just like the others, you will apologize, though you won't mean it. I know this because a weapon is a great persuader. After that everything you will do will simply be out of pity. You will see me as crazy, and reject me all over again. You will comply simply to make me feel better. I can't stand pity, and I don't want yours.

That is why we must bring this to a conclusion. That way you will be mine forever, we can skip through the usual process as I've done all of that before. I will end this before the restraining orders, before I begin to get bitter. While good memories are still young. Even now that I know things are going awry, I can still look at you with no contempt.

You may wonder now, what will become of you? I can assure you darling, just as in life you will be treated nothing like the others. I think I'll tie ribbons around cut off locks of your lovely hair. They'll make great decorations for my bedroom. Perhaps I'll put a tack through them so that they may hang above my bed. Your ribs may find their way onto my living room wall, especially close to the fireplace. That way, I will always know that your bones are warm there by the fire. Finally, I found an antique tear catcher so that your final tears could be encased in it, and that I may have you with me always.

Don't mistake me, my pet... I've never treated anyone, or their remains with such reverence. You are special, and you are mine. Even when I am done with you and we are separated more... permanently, I will still be yours. I will always be yours, with each victim that comes subsequently, even if there ever were a person who could return my affections... You will remain special among all of those who have fallen by my hand.

Love,

Your not so secret admirer

CHAPTER TEN

Rattles

"58, 59, 60" I counted. Josh took note. We moved on to the next box, this one full of electrical wires. I began counting.

It was nearing twelve o'clock at night. Inventory was tedious, the warehouse was hot and had no A.C., but we were getting paid overtime, which made it worth it. We were the only two left; everyone else was gone hours ago. There was still a lot of work to do, but we didn't mind. Every couple of hours we made a run to the nearby taco chain to keep us energized.

Suddenly, I felt the effects of one of those tacos creeping up. I started counting faster.

"125, 126, 127" I finished after a moment. Josh took note.

"I'm gonna take a dump," I said. Josh nodded. He started counting the next box himself as I walked off towards the bathroom.I opened the door to the office section of the building, where the bathrooms were. Through the large glass window I saw her, for the first time.

She was pale as snow, her hair a light, wispy blonde. She wore a thin, faintly blue dress, nearly translucent in the light of the full moon. I could see her pale, naked body under it. She was beautiful, yet scars stretched across her stomach, as if it had been cut across with a knife over and over. She lifted a finger, beckoning me.

Then, as soon as I saw her, she was gone. I shook my head and blinked, and yet saw nothing but the darkness and moonlight beyond the door.

Half sure I had saw nothing and half sure it was a trick of my mind, I turned right and went into the bathroom.I sat on the toilet and pulled out my phone. For some reason, the Internet wasn't working. "Damn wi-fi," I muttered and placed it back in my pocket. Then the hissing began.

At first it was faint, and I assumed it was only the plumbing. And yet, as it grew louder and louder it began to sound more and more like a voice –

the voice of a woman.

Suddenly, the sound was unbearably loud, and then it began – the rattling.

The handle to the stall door rattled, as if someone on the other side was trying to get in. Soon the door began to shake, and within seconds the whole stall was in convulsion.

The hissing grew only louder, and formed into words.

"Come to me," it beckoned. "Come to meeeee," it whispered into my ear.

A mixture of terror and shock had me frozen, glued to the seat. Then I looked down. Below the door I saw them – her feet. I hadn't payed much attention to her feet when I saw her before, but I knew they were hers. I knew.

"Come to meeeee."

Suddenly, in a burst of both courage and insanity, I lunged for the door, knocking into it with both fists. And everything was quiet.I stood there, breathless, staring at the door, not daring to look down. Finally my eyes dragged down to the floor.

The feet were gone. The door creaked open, seemingly of its own will. I almost left then and there. I almost bolted out of the building. But I knew I couldn't leave Josh with her in here, and knew I had no choice but to return to the warehouse.

"Josh!" I yelled at the top of my lungs, as I pushed through the door.. "Josh! We have to leave – NOW!"

I heard no reply. Terror gripped me, but I kept going.

When I made it to the end of the warehouse I saw him, hanging. His feet were tied together with electrical wire, his fingers severed. He hung upside-down from the ceiling, a pool of blood gathering beneath him. Above his pelvis, a large gash ran across his belly, and his entrails spilling from the wound. His tongue was stretched out across his face, a long, crude, rusted nail driven through it into his forehead. I couldn't move.

That's when the hissing began again – at once as loud as it was before. In the hissing I heard her whispers.

"Come to me." She said. "Come to me."

I turned around, and looked straight into her burning red eyes. Her mouth slipped open as she repeated her mantra. She extended her arms and embraced me.

I closed my eyes shut, for the final time.

CHAPTER ELEVEN

Chemical

If you asked me how long we've been down here, I wouldn't know. We don't see the sun, and nobody seems to have a watch. It doesn't matter anyway; we don't have anywhere to be. For all we know there isn't anywhere left to be. The surface has surely been overrun with death and decay by now.

There are six of us left. Until just recently there were seven. Her screaming has stopped now and I feel relief. It was hard to sleep with those agonizing screams and the banging on the steel door. Huddled in my blankets, I look around at the other survivors; four men and a woman, all of us unkempt and haggard. At one point we all worked here, but since the accident it's become our prison. The painfully low amount of food is in a pile in the center of the room, so we can all keep an eye on it to make sure nobody is taking more then we're allowed per day. There's enough food for three, maybe four meals. None of us want to think about it. We just stare.

There are no beds, just piles of blankets and paper that make crude sleeping areas. There's one bathroom at the far end of the complex and it has running water. There are three other rooms, rooms we used to work in, filled with computers and lab equipment that has accumulated a fine layer of dust. We still have power somehow, so all the security cameras and lights still work. Unfortunately none of the computers work because they've been shut and locked, as per emergency protocol. Any contact with the outside world is non-existent.

We worked for the military, doing basic chemical research. Somewhere along the line a chemical was leaked, and the results were fatal. People who came into direct contact with the chemical succumbed to vomiting, mild at first, then intense, until they had nothing to excrete except for their own blood. Nobody lasted more then a couple hours once they had touched the chemical. It also spread through saliva, bile and blood, so those with the misfortune of coming into contact with even a single drop are doomed. We had to toss that woman out because we caught her vomiting in the toilet.

She said she was pregnant and that it was only morning sickness, but you can't be sure. Her fiancé, Barry, tried to intervene, calling us animals. We clubbed him over the head, then tied and gagged him to a thick pipe at one end of the room. He strains against the bonds and screams into the gag occasionally, a fierce and wild-eyed look on is face. It's for his own good and the good of everyone here. He might hurt someone. He needs to be untied and fed eventually, but nobody wants to be the one to do it. So we just sit and stare at the pile of food on the floor that gets lower with each rationed meal. He's another mouth to feed that we can't afford.

Everyone is on edge, twitchy and jumpy. Every movement is watched intently, with suspicious and unrelenting eyes. Nobody talks anymore. They just stare. We all know we're going to die, it's just a matter of time before hunger or the chemical gets us. It's all in the backs of our minds, eating away at our sanity.

It's been awhile now since the incident with the sick woman. Barry died while I was asleep, and our food supplies have run out. I draw the blanket over my head and drift into a fitful sleep, filled with hunger pangs. I'm awakened some time later by the sound of whispers. I can see three members of our group huddled in a circle and identify them as Marcus, Daniel and Eileen.

My stirring causes them to look over, piercing me with savage eyes. They start moving towards me with a hungry look on their faces. Their intent hits me with a sudden burst of fear, and I scramble to my feet. Marcus grabs me by the collar, and it tears as I break loose from his grip. Daniel grabs at my blanket and I shove him hard against the third attacker, Eileen. They go sprawling and I spring past them and into the computer room, locking the door as fast as I can. Dragging desks and cabinets, I make a crude and hopefully secure barricade. I see them banging themselves against the door and the windows, glaring at me with feral eyes. Something catches their attention down the hall, and they stop, heads snapping sharply in the direction of the bathroom.

The fifth man, Jackson, must have finished using the facilities, unaware of the intent of the other three. He approaches and peers into the window, a puzzled look on his face. I try to scream a warning, but all that escapes my throat is a hoarse rattle. It's too late anyway, and his face is smashed against the glass by one of the others. I stare in horror as his face is smashed to a pulp, each thud resounding through the room like a slow heartbeat. Then his body is taken away and there is silence.

They're gone for now, but they'll be back. Hunger gnaws at my stomach and I search frantically for any morsel of food. With extreme luck, I manage to find a candy bar in one of the desk drawers and hungrily devour it, thanking whoever it was who had the sweet tooth. My bliss soon passes, and the hunger pains return. I try to sleep, but even the slightest sound jolts me awake. I have no idea how much time has passed but suddenly they were bashing the blood smeared window with a pipe. They're going to get in, and I will need to defend myself.

There's an emergency axe in one corner of the room, inside a glass case. I smash the glass and retrieve it, and it makes me fell a little better. My anxiety grows along the spider web cracks on the window with each passing moment. After God knows how many attempts, the window finally shatters and the wild, barely human face of Marcus peers in. I sit in a chair, with the axe out of view, and wait. I'm going to die anyway, so I might as well go out fighting. He climbs in, followed by Eileen and finally Daniel. They approach slowly, in a mini skirmish line.

When they get close enough, Marcus raises the pipe for a killing blow. Before he has time to bring it down, I swing the axe and slice him in the chest. The pipe clatters to the floor and as I spring to my feet. Eileen lunges at where I was and crashes into the now empty chair. I swing the axe, catching Daniel off guard and delivering a blow to the temple. His blood showers me and stings my eyes, blinding me. Eileen lunges for me again and tackles me around the ankles, sending me to the ground. I managed to hang on to my axe, and as her hands clasp around my neck I slash her throat. The hands grip tighter for a moment and then loosen, and her lifeless body crumples on top of me.

Pushing her off, I stagger towards Marcus, gagging from the strangling I had just received. He was still alive, dragging himself through his own blood towards the fallen pipe. I stick my foot on his back and swing the axe onto his skull. My heart racing, I stumble backwards and am grabbed by hands from behind. The axe is wrenched from my hand and I feel a sharp prick on my neck. I lose all muscle control and slump to the floor. Through blurred vision I see men in hazmat suits all around me. I hear the sound of their voices, but they seem distorted and far away. Then the man nearest me speaks and the words register into my brain with horror.

"The experiment has gone on long enough," he says, before I sink into total darkness.

CHAPTER TWELVE

Beware of Those Who Would Do You Harm – Act 2

Act 2 – Tucker

Tucker was beginning to wonder if Abby wasn't into him anymore. Ever since he tried to help her find out what happened to Wendy, she had been acting strange. They barely hung out anymore, and she was returning his calls and messages less and less. At school, she was elusive, and it seemed like she wasn't concerned about her appearance anymore.

She had always been a tomboy, preferring to wear jeans and t-shirts over skirts and high-heels. But there was something different now; now her outfits looked thrown together instead of having some sort of cohesion. And her hair, it was like she hadn't combed it in months. It wasn't like he really cared about how she looked, but he knew that something terrible must have happened. Did it have something to do with Wendy?

But worse than all of that, she was always acting like someone was following her. Once, when he went over to her house to hang out, she insisted that they close all of the curtains and double check the locks on every single window and door. He had suggested watching a movie, but when he put it on she was watching anything but. Abby kept glancing back and forth between the TV and the hallway, like someone would be walking through there at any moment. Not to mention that she jumped at every sound and her mind seemed elsewhere. When she would look at him, he felt like she was looking right through him.

If she was in some kind of trouble, he needed to know. He hated feeling like he couldn't protect her, and after all, there was still a killer at large. Granted, Jeff might be long gone if he knew what was good for him. Still, Wendy was missing, and Jeff may have had something to do with it. Tucker decided to stop by her house after school to confront her about what was going on. It had been three weeks since he hacked into Wendy's computer for her, and since then he has heard no more talk about finding her from Abby.

As Tucker was about to leave his house for Abby's, he heard the phone ring. He considered ignoring it, but then he remembered that his parents were out for a date night. He dashed into the kitchen and picked it up on the fourth ring.

"Hello?"

"Hello, Tucker?"

"Abby is that you? I was just about to come over."

"No, don't come over."

"Why not!? You've been acting so weird lately. Are we even still together?"

There was a pause and he heard her take a deep breath.

"I'm really sorry, Tuck. I just...I made a mistake."

"What mistake?" Tucker asked, desperate.

"It doesn't matter. I just wanted to let you know that I love you. And also, thank you for everything."

"I love you too but what's going on Abby? Is this about Wendy? Have you found her? Is she coming back?"

There was another pause, and then: "I don't think she's ever coming back, Tuck."

"What? Why?"

"No matter what happens Tuck, no matter what, don't come looking for me. Don't ask questions. I want you to keep on living, and have a good life."

"What are you talking about? Where are you going? Abby!"

"Goodbye Tucker, I love you."

"Abby wait–!"

But she had already hung up. Tucker slowly put the phone back on the receiver and slumped against the wall. He couldn't be sure; maybe his mind was playing tricks on him. Right before Abby hung up the phone, he thought he heard an ominous male voice chuckling in the background.

Tucker wasted no time jumping into his 1999 Chevy Silverado and speeding over to Abby's place. It only takes about five minutes to get to her house from his, so when he got there and banged on the door, he was surprised when no one answered.

Tucker looked through the window next to the door, but the house was completely dark. He called out to her, but still, there was no answer. He ran around to the side of the house, and even to the back door, but he couldn't see or hear anything. She was gone.After waiting almost an hour on her doorstep, Tucker scribbled a note on some mail using a pen he happened to have in his truck. When he got home, he waited for hours. But she never called him. Finally, he decided to call her and really lay into her.

"Hello?"

"Hi, this is Tucker. May I speak to Abby?"

"I'm sorry Tuck, she isn't home. In fact, I thought she would be with you."

"No ma'am, I haven't seen her since we talked earlier."

"Well that's strange; I wonder where she could be."

Tucker paused for a moment. Then:

"I don't mean to alarm you ma'am, but I think you should call the police."

It was Wendy all over again. Abby had simply vanished, and no one knew why. Some people wondered if she had gone to find Wendy, others were convinced that her disappearance was linked to the other disappearances happening around town. But a smaller percentage, including Tucker, believed that a certain killer was the culprit. And Tucker was determined to find out if his suspicions were true.

Tucker wasn't the only one who wanted answers. Abby's parents were sick with worry, and they exhausted every resource possible in order to find her. They called the police station daily demanding any news that they had. They even had the police go through Abby's things, unlike Wendy. What the police couldn't understand was why, just like with Wendy, none of her things were missing. It was as if she had just gotten up and walked out. There was no note, no clues, nothing.

By the time a month had gone by, the police were ready to give up their search and label her as a runaway despite the evidence against that claim. Her parents were frantic. As time went on, they felt more and more alone in their search. Search parties and calls with information were occurring less and the police began to brush them off. They were never the best police force anyway, because nothing really happened in that town. But there was one other person who was not ready to give up.

Tucker began his own little investigation, beginning with asking after her around town. He picked a Saturday morning to begin, and by that Saturday afternoon he had gotten nowhere. No one had seen her the day she disappeared, no one had even seen her around that time because she barely went anywhere besides school in those last few weeks. Tucker was wondering what he should do next when he realized something. The day when everything changed was the same day that he had hacked into Wendy's computer. There must have been something important on there that she had found after he left. He realized that he would have to go back to her house and find out what it was.

Instead of driving over to her house, he left his car at his house and jogged over to Abby's. He kept in constant contact with her parents, so he knew that Saturdays were when they both went out to do what they could to find their daughter, whether its search for her, hand out flyers, or haunt the police station for any leads.

Once he got there, he found the extra key hidden in a flowerpot and headed up to her room. Glancing at the clock and noting the time, he quickly went to work. Instead of searching through Wendy's computer like he had originally planned, he instead logged onto Abby's. He never told her this, but he knew all of he login information because she wasn't as careful as she should have been while typing it in.

There wasn't much on her computer, but there were tons of searches about the old house out in the cornfields. It looked like she was wondering if you could get Internet connection from out there. Puzzled, Tucker checked through her files and there he found tons of pictures of the old house. Tucker began to wonder if that's where Wendy and Abby were hiding. But, why? He decided he would check it out later. But first, he would check her emails to see if she had been communicating with anyone, besides him.

Upon looking through her emails, he found nothing. Just the dozen or so emails he had sent to her that went unanswered and some other junk. But just as he was about to close out, he caught sight of her spam folder. After considering it, he decided that it wouldn't do any harm just to check.

All of the messages were from an anonymous sender.

"Okay...that's weird." He muttered.

Tucker decided to choose one at random.

You were warned, but you just couldn't help yourself. And now you know too much.

Tucker narrowed his eyes at the screen. Then he clicked on another, more recent one.

Jeffrey's coming to get you, Abby dear. You'd better not tell.

Tucker clinched his fists and turned away from the computer. "Jeff." He said through his teeth, voice dripping with venom. Turning back to the computer, he clicked on a few more. Piecing together most of the emails,

Tucker figured Abby had found out something about Jeff, and now Jeff was coming for her. He also knew in his gut that it had something to do with Wendy.

"She better not be dead, you fucker..." Tucker muttered as he held his head in his hands. Fresh tears rolled down his cheeks, he didn't want to admit what he already knew was true. "I'll find you Jeff, I swear I'll–!" Then, it hit him. A simple connection; the common denominator. Of course Jeff had never left; he had been living right under everyone's noses this whole time. Tucker clicked out of her email and went brought up the window that he had used to search Abby's most recent history. He brought up the most recent search, and there it was. The place where Wendy was found shivering in the darkness, the place that Abby had become obsessed with, the place where no one would think to look. The old abandoned house in the cornfields, that's were Jeff was.

Tucker didn't stop to think. Instead, almost in a trance-like state, he put everything back in order, and left the room. When he got home, he wrote a goodbye letter to his parents, telling them that he loved them, and that he was leaving to be with Abby. He wrote it, knowing that he may never return. Some don't come back when they set off to confront evil.

Tucker pushed his way through the cornfields. He knew the way to the house like the back of his hand. He shook away the thoughts that tried to force their way into his head of him, Abby, and other neighborhood kids playing out here when they were younger. No distractions. They could still be alive, though the chance was slim. Either way, he needed to know everything, or else he would never find peace.

It wasn't long before he could see the dark house looming before him. Once he had stepped onto the porch, he took a deep breath, and reached for the doorknob.

"Run."

Tucker whirled around, but there was nothing there but the cornfields from whence he came.

"Abby?" He whispered. He could have sworn he had heard her just now. But that was impossible. It must have been his imagination, or the wind whispering through the fields. Or maybe it was his subconscious crying out for him to get as far way from this place as he could, and it took on the voice of the person who was always on his mind. But it was too late; he was here now. And the fear that gripped him and shook him to the bone was not enough to stop him. Once again he closed his eyes, took a deep breath, and opened the door.

The smell of death and rot immediately slapped him in the face and forced him to take a step back. It was so strong that he actually gagged and had to force himself not to throw up. Despite the overwhelming smell, he stumbled into the dark house and tried to find his way around. The house had two stories, including a basement and an attic.

He knew that Jeff was most likely on the second floor, that's where all of the bedrooms were. Tucker closed his eyes as he tried not to think about all the times that he and Abby had snuck out here to make out in the master bedroom. Strangely enough, the house was fully furnished with ancient furniture and old photographs. It was the perfect place for a killer to hang around. But there was no electricity, so how in the world could he survive here.

Darkness. He was a creature of the darkness, that's why.

After finding the stairway, he started to climb it only to slip on some sort of dark liquid. Luckily he caught himself on the railing, but that also was covered in warm liquid. Tucker quickly pulled his hand away, knowing what it very well could be. He tiptoed up the stairs but stopped at the top. He cocked his head to the side and listened. There was a sound coming from his right. A very distinct sound, like something heavy was being dragged across the floor. Tucker gulped and headed towards the sound. Eventually, he could see a flickering light coming from a room at the end of the hallway. There was also what Tucker assumed to be a blood trail and bloody footprints leading into that room.

The dragging sound got louder as he reached the door. Tucker leaned against the wall next to the doorway and composed himself. He wanted so badly to bide his time and wait for the police, whom he had called right before heading out. They had sounded skeptical, and he knew that they would probably take their time in getting there. A killer right under their noses, and in the most obvious place this whole time? Yeah, right. Still, he was sure they would come. But he couldn't wait for whenever that may be at the risk of Jeff escaping. So with a trembling heart, he turned and stepped into the room.

The room looked like any other bedroom, except for a few things. For one, there was nothing in it but a large bed, a desk with a computer and one candle on it, and another, smaller, doorway. From what Tucker could make out in the dim light, the walls and floor were covered in splotches of blood, some of them spelling out actual words. Tucker couldn't read what the words said, but it wasn't important to him at the moment. What was important, were the two figures in the room that had stopped moving as soon as he stepped in.

The first figure he saw was a young woman lying on the floor. She was dead, her body nearly cut in two and its contents spilling out around her. He could see her empty eyes in the candlelight, wide and staring. She looked to be very beautiful, with long bloodstained blonde hair and grey eyes. Her hand was being held in another hand, belonging to the one who had dragged her broken body all the way up the stairs to this very room. It seemed to be in the middle of dragging her to the second door, because its hand had frozen in the middle of reaching for the doorknob. This figure was standing just out of the candles range, so it was consumed by shadows. But Tucker knew exactly who it was.

"Jeff."

The figure dropped the girl's hand and let the other hand fall to its side. It just stood there for a moment, and then it began to chuckle quietly.

"So...I see you didn't take her warning to heart hmmm...?" came a voice that sounded like it would better suit a serpent than a human being.Tucker flinched at the sound of that voice. It sounded much more malicious than what he remembered, but he could still tell who it belonged to.

"What have you done with her!" he demanded, sounding much more confidant than he actually was.

"You should have stayed away...heheh...I might have left you alone. But now..."

"Stop fucking around and answer my goddamned question!"

The figure was silent for a moment. Then he stepped over the corpse and into the light. Tucker sucked in a breath as he saw Jeff for the first time in months. The boy he had known in school was normal compared to the creature that stood before him now. The long unkempt black hair and bone white skin were still the same, but now his face was horribly disfigured.

His eyelids were gone, leaving behind emotionless eyes with black rings around them that seemed to stare right into Tucker's soul. His nose was gone too, but for some reason there was no hole where it used to be, just a small white hump. His lips were also gone, so now he no longer needed Joker make-up to give himself a permanent smile. His clothes were the same though, a white hoodie with fresh blood on it, and black pants.

"Jesus Christ...what happened to you?" Tucker asked, more than a little shaken.

"What happened?" Jeff cocked his head back and let out a throaty laugh that sent chills down Tuckers spine. "SHE happened!" He said at last.

"Wendy?"

Jeff said nothing.

"Why did you take her? Why did you kill her parents? Why did you...what did you do to Abby!?"

Jeff cocked his head to the side and his evil grin seemed to grow wider.

"You want answers hmmm...? Well...I guess I can confide in you...since you won't be around for much longer."

Tucker wondered if he should just run. If he left now he might be able to make it out of there alive. But he couldn't, he needed to know. Besides, the police should be on their way by now, right? . Instead of immediately talking, Jeff casually turned and picked up the girl from the floor and placed her on the bed, careful not to spill anything. He then sat down at his desk and faced Tucker, who still remained in the doorway.

"I'll have some fun with her later...heheh. Now where should I begin? Oh yes, ever since I was twelve, I've had these urges. The urge to kill, specifically. I loved it, and ever since my first kill I've been dying to do it more and more and more! It gave me joy like no other to take someone's life, that is, until I came here."

Tucker was only mildly interested in what he had to say. He wasn't at all surprised that Jeff was psychotic. He only wanted to stall, and find out if his Abby was still alive. But then he thought maybe there was a way he could take down Jeff himself, so he decided to listen more carefully.

"As you could imagine, for six years I've been on the run from my past. I'd travel from city to city, have my fill of fun, then move on. When I got here, it was easy to make up some bullshit story about living with my great aunt. In reality I just hid out at some rich old bitch's house who I had kept hostage...for a while."

Tucker stopped himself from rolling his eyes. He absolutely hated Jeff, a person who would kill without remorse or regard for someone's life. But in order to find out what happened, he had to keep listening.

"I enrolled myself in school to scout some potential victims." Jeff went on. "I usually try to pick people who I can gain something from. But then I met Wendy. She came frolicking into my life without warning, and suddenly everything changed. She was changing me. At first I fancied her as my first victim here, but I actually began to...fall for her. Several times I tried to kill her, the first time being after we had sex for the first time. She lay there, fast asleep, and I straddled her and pulled the knife out from underneath the pillow. But as I raised the knife to stab her in the heart, I hesitated. I saw how beautiful she looked sleeping so peacefully, and I hesitated."

Tucker noted how Jeff's voice had changed over the course of him telling this story. He almost sounded normal. Like a normal person struggling with their feelings. Too bad he wasn't a normal person, and this wasn't a normal love story.

"I hated myself for it, I was starting to slip. I went out on killing sprees less and less, and began to spend more time with her. The second time I was planning to kill her, she told me she loved me, and I couldn't bring myself to use the axe I had hidden underneath the table to hack her to pieces. And the third time... I was really going to do it."

Tucker perked up again at the change of tone in Jeff's voice. He figured he knew what story Jeff was about to tell now.

"I had to get rid of her, so that I would be able to freely do what I wanted. I couldn't allow myself to have feelings for her. It was changing me and I didn't like it! So I planned everything out so nothing would go wrong this time. While she was out partying, I killed her parents then waited for her to come home. When she got there, oh, her face was priceless. It filled my heart with such glee to see her in so much pain. Yes, the feeling was back again. I knew I could do it this time! I followed her all the way here, wounding her in the process. I didn't want any chances for her to escape, so I made sure she wouldn't be able to run far."

Tucker nodded solemnly, remembering the wound on the back of Wendy's knee that never quite healed, just like her broken heart.

"I was so ready to end her, but then..." Jeff scratched his arm and twitched nervously. "Then she kissed me, and the urge was completely gone. It was such a shock that I couldn't do anything, I just had to get away from her."

Tucker shook his head. If only you had just let it change you. You could have been happy with her. But instead...

"I went back to the old lady's house. I couldn't stay there long because the smell coming from her basement was starting to bug the neighbors. I looked at myself in the mirror and cursed myself for being so weak. I knew I had to do something drastic, think...think...THINK! And then I knew: it was my lips that had betrayed me. I had to get rid of them, so I did. And while I was at it, why not punish myself further? I burned off my eyelids I had no real use for them, and now I would never lose sight of my desires!" Jeff's serpent-like voice had returned by now.

"And your nose?" Tucker asked, grimly.

"Just an added bonus, to seal the deal." Jeff then stood up, and looked Tucker square in the face. "There was nothing stopping me anymore. I was transformed; I just needed to do one more thing to make sure I never went back. This time I kept a safe distance from her. Instead I sent her threatening emails, and stalked her at night. I wanted to weaken her resolve by slowly driving her insane. And it worked; by the time I was through with her, she had no will to live and accepted her fate without a struggle. I had won."

Tucker glared at him. "What did you do to her?"

"What do you think?" Jeff said, teasingly. "I...took her."

Tucker took an angry step forward, but immediately regretted it. "And Abby? Why did you go after her?"

"She went investigating, just like I knew she would, and found out too much. I did the same to her, only she was much stronger than Wendy. Sill, she eventually realized she couldn't escape from me. Should have heeded Wendy's warning...hmmm?"

Tucker felt sick. His head began to swim, and he swayed back and forth on his feet. How could something so evil exist in this world? By this time, he knew they were dead, but still he had to ask once more.

"Where are they? Where are Abby and Wendy now?"

Jeff's unholy grin grew so wide that it nearly split his face in half and he gestured around the room.

"Why...they're here." Jeff produced a large knife from the pocket of his hoodie and advanced toward him. Tucker knew what that meant. It meant that the police weren't going to make it in time after all. Instead of running, like his subconscious was currently screaming for him to do, he simply closed his eyes and thought of Abby.

"They're right here with us." Jeff went on, is a harsh whisper. "You can see them if you want. All you have to do is GO TO SLEEP!"

CHAPTER THIRTEEN

The Stalker

Leslie sat on the barstool, sipping a margarita. She'd hit a run of bad luck in the past few months. First her boyfriend Ricky left her, then she lost her job. She got a new job, but not as well paying, of course. So she had to move out of her house and into a cramped apartment.

Her cat, Muffin, died. Her mother was ill, and needed her support, even though she couldn't support herself. With all that bad luck, its little wonder that she let that guy sit next to her, buy her a drink, the same old routine. The fella's name was Geoffry. He seemed nice enough, even if he was kind of a dweeb. He wore horn-rimmed glasses with a blue button down shirt, he wasn't nerd-skinny, exactly, but he was kind of on the thin side.

They talked for awhile, and then she left the bar. The next day, as she was walking home from work, Leslie saw Geoffry again, standing at the bus stop a block away from her office building. "Hi, Leslie! Hey I was thinking maybe we could head down to the bar tonight. I really had fun last night." She politely declined, and he said, "Okay, well, I'll see you again."

She left for work the next day, and guess who she saw? Geoffry was standing right there about a block from her house. "Hi Leslie! You wanna hook up tonight? I was thinking maybe a movie?" She politely declined, and went about her work. When she got home, she had a new message on the answering machine. [Hi, Leslie! It's me, Geoffry. I just thought you might've changed your mind about the movies. Don't make me keep asking, just call me, bye!]

The next morning, Leslie left for work. Geoffry was standing outside her door. "Hi Leslie! Why'd you stand me up last night, huh? I just want a chance, Leslie, we can try, right?" After 3 days of annoyance, Leslie caved. "Fine, Geoffry, we can try. Why don't you come over for dinner tomorrow night? We'll see how it goes, okay?"

Leslie sure was having a bad run of luck. Ricky was in hysterics when he left her, her cat was dead, and now Geoffry too. What was left of his corpse was found a week later...

(I accidentally deleted this post when I was clearing out stuff by a certain author, I'm sorry... but it's back now... I backdated it so hopefully it won't pop up in your RSS feeds again, if it did, I'm sorry)

CHAPTER FOURTEEN

In Between

I'm in between.

One of them bit me. The bastard took a chunk out of my upper arm. The fool probably didn't even know it was an arm. He probably saw me as a walking turkey leg or something. Oh, but he got his dues. I whacked his useless head off with a crowbar I stole when shit got serious.

It got serious about a month ago, and let me tell you, it happened just the way everyone thought it would happen. Some "contained" little outbreak, then BOOM, everyone I know is staggering around like kangaroos tripping on dextro. Not me, though. I knew I was going to fight it. I did well until about a week ago when Mr. Slobbermouth munched on my bicep.

It amazes even me that I'm so coherent. God, I wish I wasn't. I'm not like them, but I'm just like them. I have the hunger they have, but I have all the guilt and love of humanity that is going to keep me from surviving.I'm not even sure that I want to survive anymore. I see them do horrible things, things that are starting to drive me mad, and I either get sick to my stomach or find my mouth watering. I don't want to live if living means I have to watch the destruction of my kind every day.

But then, this means no more hiding. It's as if they can sense something in me, like they scan for a zombie membership card and find it on me. They leave me alone. I can walk freely among them.

You know how I said I'm just like them? Well, I'm better than them. I'm smarter and have the ability to gain the trust of humans. I found one yesterday, I know where all the good hiding spots are, you see, and Lord was it happy to see me. It grasped my arm and looked into my eyes, saying it was happy to have found someone to fight with. Making sure none of the no-brains were around, I took it with me and hid with it in a storm cellar. I let it fall asleep, then I broke its neck, busted open its head like a coconut, and tore into its meaty brain. The blood complimented it nicely.

For a few moments, I felt bad for what I had done. I saw his body in that stagnant pool of blood, looking as if he was still sleeping, and felt some remorse for the poor, trusting boy. I wondered about his life before the disaster. Was he happy? Did his family love him? Would he have survived anyway?

That acidic guilt rose in me, a constant reminder of my humanity. But there's at least one thing zombies and humans have in common: the will to survive. And I'm about to do a much better job than either one of them will.

CHAPTER FIFTEEN

Confession

I grew up in Royal Oak, Michigan, about twenty minutes from downtown Detroit. It's one of those places where the people with money ran to after things in the city went shit-shaped.

I went to high school with this guy I'll call Nick. We had a TV Production class together, and we both decided that was the kind of thing we wanted to do for a living, so we ended up in a lot of the same film classes in college.

We weren't that close, and I didn't hang out with him that much outside of school, but a year after graduation, he contacted me about this show he wanted to make. He said he really liked my camera work, and I was better with editing and effects programs than most of the other students – I'd been playing with them as a hobby since tenth grade – and he said he could use my knowledge for the production values.

Nick was never that great at the technical side of things. Even after film school, his stuff always looked kind of cheap and Youtube-y. But he was charming, the kind of guy who could do great voiceovers, come up with impressive-sounding "artistic visions" (he was great at putting on airs and convincing stupid people his shitty-looking films were actually high art with all kinds of symbolic metaphorical ironic subtext or whatever) and pitch the hell out of any idea, no matter how stupid. So he thought we'd make a good team.

His idea was for this "Real Stories of Detroit" type of show. I mean, That wasn't what he called it, but it's a pretty good summary of the premise. His explanation was that people on the outside know this place sucks, but besides all those dilapidated building photos ("ruin porn, " they call it) and the crime reports no one cares about, they don't know enough about the very real horror that happens here on a daily basis. In other words, they didn't see us as human, man, just a big joke.

I agreed with some of his points, I wasn't finding paying work at the time, and I wanted to help out an old sort-of-friend, so I agreed to do some camera work for him. If anything became of it, I'd get partial credit and we'd split the profits.

During the planning phase, Nick was always going on about how the show would have both artistic merit and social relevance, exposing the darker side of humanity as well as the conditions we overlook right here in America, and hopefully, encourage the complacent masses to wake up and do something about our poverty and urban blight.

It took me about a week to realize that was all bullshit.

In the early days, the material that would make up the meat of our show was hard to find, so we spent hours every day combing through shock and gore sites for whatever we could find that might have come from around here in the last ten years. Over the next several months, my external drive filled up with camcorder videos of rotting corpses people stumbled across, security camera footage of cashiers getting shot in the face by robbers, leaked footage of blood-soaked crime scenes, and every type of forensic photo imaginable.

We called up and interviewed crack whores – the very few who had access to phones and could complete intelligible sentences, anyway – ex-cons, and people who'd confess to any depraved shit as long as we didn't show their faces. The "real stories" were never positive, always just the worst shit we could dig up. We never talked to people reading storybooks to kids or tending community gardens or anything.

According to Nick, that was "feel-good fluff" and didn't "reflect the city's brutal reality."

According to Nick, what did "reflect the city's brutal reality" was a freak show of poverty, misery, and suffering.

We added some dramatic public domain music and somber narration, but that was the only thing "artistic" about it. Our first episode was too gory for any TV network to touch, or to post on any of the big video hosting sites without it getting pulled within the week. But we started our own site, and Nick posted links on a few of the sites where we'd found our source material.

It took a less than a month for me to start hating it, but when I make promises, I keep them.

I didn't really want to quit until after what happened to J.J.

We did a lot of shooting on the streets – for both the interviews and for ruin porn – especially in the northeast and Highland Park. If you don't know, Detroit's west side is (mostly kind of almost) a normal city. Those parts of town where you hear about the forest reclaiming whole blocks and bears wandering the streets are up Northeast. And Highland Park is the worst of the many neighborhoods that make up crackland.

None of them are the kinds of places you want to walk into unarmed with a camera, so for security, we hired this big guy with tattoos on his face who always carried a 45. I have no idea how Nick met this guy.

One day, while we were out getting footage of the old Grande Ballroom to use as establishing shots for a nearby neighborhood where I think someone set his girlfriend on fire, we met this old homeless guy who went by "J.J."

He was a drunk, but at least he wasn't on anything harder, and for a drunk, he was surprisingly friendly, lucid and intelligent.

For a few dollars an hour and some hot food, he'd show us around his stomping grounds and point out some of the more interesting sights. There was one time when he showed us a house where whoever lived there had left their doll collection behind when they moved out, for example.

Whenever we were on set, Nick was really adamant that I not only turn off my phone, but leave it at home. He wanted to make sure I didn't sneak and start texting or something while we were working.I didn't know why he was so paranoid about it at the time, I mean, it's not like he was even paying me by the hour, but it started to make perfect sense about two weeks later.

One day we were filming on Robinwood St. – just getting some shots of garbage and burnt-out houses to fill some space between videos of murders – when J.J. told us he used to squat over here, and he knew an abandoned but still pretty solid two-story house where you could get to the roof through one of the upper story windows. From there, we could get a shot of most of the neighborhood. I didn't think it was safe, even with my lightest camera, so he volunteered to go first just to show us nothing would collapse under his weight.

Well, he caught his foot on something, lost his balance, and fell right off the roof and landed in (what was left of) the concrete driveway. Both his legs snapped under him.

We both kind of panicked. Mostly because we couldn't afford to pay any medical bills or risk having anyone sue us. Nick was very adamant about that.

So we left him there.

Actually, it's a bit more complicated than that.

It quickly dawned on us that if anyone came around and found him, he'd talk to some kind of authorities as soon as he was back to civilization.Or at least I think I think that's why we decided to do it. It was hard to hear each other over all J.J.'s screaming and crying. I'd never heard a man make that much noise.

So Nick had our bodyguard hold the guy's arms while he shoved a rag into his mouth.

We used a clean one. We're not animals.

Then he duct taped it shut. Nick and I put on our gloves, so we wouldn't leave fingerprints. When we're out shooting, we carry thick work gloves everywhere we go. There's no specific reason, just that when you work in abandoned buildings, and sometimes around human waste and dead bodies, gloves are always a good thing to have. I didn't know why Nick had duct tape. Maybe it was in case he ever had to do something like that.

That muffled the screams were enough to the point where no one more than ten or twenty feet away would hear them, but Jesus, his eyes. I still have nightmares about his eyes. Bloodshot and wild with pain and terror, just begging us not to do that.

Then we bound his arms behind his back and wrapped his hands in cocoons of duct tape. Then we picked him up and moved him into a nearby abandoned house, and because he was still thrashing around, we "accidentally" let him fall down the basement stairs, so he couldn't wriggle his way out to the street.

Then we left him there.

We'd thought about having our guard just shoot him, but we all agreed that would make too much noise, and we're not murderers, we're just... Refusing to take responsibility for J.J.'s reckless actions. Yeah, something like that.

"What if we get caught?" I asked Nick.

I imagined myself trying to explain this.

The duct tape was because he was drunk and trying to attack us, officer. Had to restrain him. We're so sorry we forgot to call you, but we were just terrified.

He just looked at me like he couldn't believe my stupidity and told me they'd never investigate this. As far as they're concerned, a homeless guy just pissed off some thug who broke his legs. Happens all the time around here.

Being a human with a functioning soul, I was freaked out the entire time, and I told Nick I wanted to quit. He just shook his head.

I looked behind him, and our bodyguard was just silently staring at me, with his shirt pulled up so you could see the gun and this look devoid of any recognizable emotions on his face. He just stared me down for thirty seconds straight without breaking eye contact before I just mumbled that maybe I'd keep working here, but I'd like the rest of the day off.

Would we actually have had to pay J.J.'s hospital bills or risk a lawsuit from this man who obviously couldn't afford a lawyer? In hindsight, I don't know, and I'm pretty sure Nick didn't care.

When I got home and checked my phone, I found a text from Nick saying "SEE YOU TOMORROW."

Caps his, not mine.

I knew what that meant. I wasn't going anywhere. Nick and our bodyguard had voted down my decision, and they knew where I lived.We'd come back a few times over the next few days just to... Check up on J.J. It took about three days for him to stop moving.

After that, we went right back to making the episode, and many more after that, like nothing happened.

We developed a cult following. Teens loved what we were doing. They passed it around on Facebook, used it to gross each other out. So did that specific set of gorehounds for who slasher movies are just a little too fictional to be scary. And violence fetishists. We got a lot of comments about people jacking off to parts of our shows I never wanted to know anyone could possibly jack off to. ...And even more from people who just thought this kind of stuff was "what those ****** deserve."

This went on for almost a year without incident.

...Until, a few weeks ago, I finally admitted one of my friends in private that I'd never wanted any of this shit and part of me had always thought just moving to another state and being done with it. I'm assuming she told someone who told someone else until Nick caught wind of it somehow, because two days later, he told me we'd be filming something special.

He took me into this abandoned school in one of those neighborhoods with like one building left per block. Our bodyguard was waiting there for us, as well as about ten of his friends. They were all wearing matching colors and bandanas that covered their faces.

When I came in, Nick had set up a tripod for me, about ten feet in front of something under a filthy sheet that squirmed from time to time.

Our bodyguard pulled off the sheet, and there was this terrified kid bound, gagged, and tied to a chair. Looked like he was in his mid teens, definitely not older than twenty. He looked kind of like my little brother, and maybe that's why Nick was so enthusiastic about making me film this.

This boy, our bodyguard told us, had been talking too much, and these guys wanted to make sure the world knew just what happens to people like that. The whole time, Nick was just staring vacantly at me with this empty half-smile on his face.

I pointed the camera at the kid, turned it on, and just watched. I knew what was going to happen, but for some reason, the part of me that usually triggers fear just didn't go off.

One of the bandanas was slowly circling him, tapping a baseball bat on the floor. I think he was the leader, so he got to go first. With every tap, the kid would almost shit himself, which was the point.

Finally, after about three or four minutes of that, he swung it right into the kid's gut. They started low so he wouldn't pass out.After they'd worked over every part of the kid's body besides his head, they finally handed it back to the leader, and he took one hard, climactic swing that splattered red and bits of meat across the walls. Then several more, just to drive the point home.

By the time they were done, his face wasn't recognizable as human, I could see the white of the inside of his skull, his brain was lying on the floor looking like a raw hamburger dropped off a building, and there was a river of blood running across the floor.

The strangest part was that I didn't cry or anything. I guess that by that point, I'd just kind of checked out mentally. That was probably the moment I learned where Nick and our bodyguard got those weird stares.

When we put the footage in our show, we told everyone a gang member had anonymously dropped it in our mail slot after he heard about the kind of show we were doing.

"The following video is real, and extremely graphic. Viewer discretion is advised."

Everyone knows that just makes you want to watch it more.

As soon as I got home, I opened my email to find one from Nick saying "SEE YOU TOMORROW." That's just his way of rubbing it in.But he didn't need to, because I wasn't really planning to quit anymore. It's just something

I bitch about sometimes.

See, Nick might not have a conscience, but at least he's been unusually honest through this whole thing. He made good on his promise about the money and the credit. I'm now half-owner of what looks like it's going to be an online empire. Nick knows a lot of people, and these days, I've started to, too. Through these people, we get material.

A lot of the things it used to take us hours to dig off the internet, now... I'll get an anonymous phone call, drive out to some abandoned building where guys in masks or bandanas are waiting for me, and film, silently and without empathy, myself.

People send us even more, too, from grainy cell phone videos to almost professional-level Canon TSi work. Beatings, rape, stabbings, execution-style shootings, and some things much more creative.

It's not hard to find our site on your own, if you haven't already, but I can't link you to it. I can't even tell you its name. Nick's kind of a narcissist, and he Googles it all the time to see what people are saying about us. The site is down right now anyway. We're moving to a bigger server. All the views keep crashing it.

Local newspapers slam us and the tourist board clucks their tongues, but we bring in enough ad revenue to pay for a middle-class lifestyle for us both. One night while we were out drinking, Nick started raving about "This is what the news was talking about, the 'user-created content revolution.' We're a fuckin' Alger story, and watch, people like us are going to run the media in the future."

And it's true.

People like us will bend public opinion to our will, tell you who to vote for, and train you to love watching what we want you to see.

We'll raise your kids.

People love us. They're imitating our format all over the place. First just in this country, in places like Newark, New Orleans, and Chicago, but I'm seeing it from other ones, too. They send me all the links. Today, I watched a bunch of Zetas pick up machetes and lay into a housewife as some kid imitated Nick's narration style in Spanish.

But none of this matters. The only reason I can confess it all here is because you'll never take it seriously. Even if you've seen our site, you think it's just a spooky story to tell on the internet, and you'll assume there's no way I'm not really who I am. People have pretended to be me on the internet before. We're a legitimate company, you'll say. We'd never do things like this.

Police have questioned us a few times about stuff we may have seen, but we just tell them we find it on the internet, or it gets sent anonymously to us. No idea where this stuff comes from. Fucked-up place, this city. We have part of our budget set aside to pay off the ones who ask too many questions, and that deals with the problem. They are, after all, Detroit cops.

I don't care anymore.

CHAPTER SIXTEEN

Glass Gallery

Last week, when I was working my shift at the local museum, something happened to me. Something that can only be described as an unspeakable horror. I will try and recount it to the best of my ability, although I already feel the shackles of suppression pulling on the memory, trying to bury it as down deep into my subconscious as possible. Maybe if I get this off my chest, I'll be able to get some sleep.

I was at my post with a fellow coworker. We were stationed in front of the brand new Glass Gallery. The gallery was only open for a week at our museum because it was a traveling collection. Needless to say, there was an implacable rush of people coming to see the pieces in the exhibit. And for right reason; I had never seen such impressive glasswork in my entire life. The last groups of viewers were making their rounds through the gallery on the closing night of the exhibit, and my coworker and I were bidding them all a goodnight. Just as the last of the guests were exiting, a strange, elderly man walked through the front door of the museum and approached us.

He looked as though he was sobbing. His lower lip was trembling, his eyes were red and puffy, his voice was shaky and fragmented. But most peculiarly, he kept repeating the same damned phrase.

"I'm so afraid I'm going to break something."

It was difficult to make out what he was saying the first few times between the whimpers, but he was like a broken record; he never stopped repeating that line.

He moved slowly in a crooked, awkward sort of way.

I tried to tell him that the gallery was closing up and that he probably wouldn't have enough time to appreciate the pieces, but it seemed as though he didn't hear a word I said. He just kept sobbing his sad line, and limped right on through the entrance to the gallery. I looked at my coworker, and he just shrugged at me.

I could hear the words "going to break something" fade as the old man walked deeper and deeper into the exhibit. After about five minutes, when every other patron had left, my coworker said he was going to go check on the old man. At this point, he was the last guest in the gallery, and I think we both were a little concerned about a crooked old man alone amongst millions of dollars' worth of art. Maybe he actually would break something.

My coworker disappeared, and I stood at the entrance for what felt like forever. Neither the old man nor my coworker resurfaced. Confused, a little worried even, I decided to go into the gallery myself and see what was going on. I walked my path with slight pace, not leaving the pieces unnoticed. It really would be a shame if one of these were to break; they were gorgeous.

I turned the corner and continued through the exhibit. I didn't see either my coworker or the old man. I kept walking.

There was one more turn in the gallery before it looped back around to the exit. As I approached the corner, I slowly started to hear sobbing, no, crying. My heart started to beat faster, and I noticed that I broke out almost into a run.

The crying increased. The corner was about five or six feet away from me. There were no windows in the gallery, and the head lights had gone off. The only lighting in the entire corridor was that of those illuminating the individual pieces, baking them in an orange glow. Around the corner, a similar type of orange glow cast a shadow on the floor, and I could see the crooked silhouette of the old man. I remember thinking that he looked at lot more crooked than the first time I saw him. And then I turned the corner.

Standing there, almost right in front of me, was the old man, crying harder than I remember. But there was something different about him. He wasn't repeating that phrase any longer. He was whimpering something else that I couldn't quite make out. I decided to look past him, and then I saw it, what was making that shadow on the floor.

I saw my coworker. He was lying on the floor. His face was in a freeze frame of anguish. But his back. His back. His back. It was snapped at a disturbingly unnatural angle. It looked like his spine had been severed in half. His legs were pointing in one direction, and his torso was pointing in another one entirely. He was quivering. Horrified, I looked away, unable to conjure a single word. I then heard what the old man was saying.

Between his bouts of tears and breathlessness, between his cries and wails, the words he was now saying were, "I did it. I broke something."

CHAPTER SEVENTEEN

Arthur

You volunteer at the mental health clinic. Given the dangerous nature of the residents, they assigned you the rooms of the less violent patients. The suicidal. Those who hear voices. Those that don't say anything at all.

You become close to a mute man named Arthur. He is a rapt listener, willing to nod his head for hours as you tell him the story of your life. You mention your past, your present. The people involved in both. Your hopes for the future.

And Arthur just nods.

After several months of listening, you figure that you owe it to Arthur to get him out of the clinic. He can't be happy sitting in a room by himself nodding at interns everyday. You talk to the supervisor of the clinic. You argue that he isn't harming anyone. That he grooms and feeds himself with no problems. That perhaps his condition is a physical aliment.

The day comes when your arguing pays off. The supervisor has agreed to let Arthur go. You rush to his room to tell him the news. "You're free!" You shout. "Isn't that great?"

And Arthur just nods.

You write your name and address on a piece of paper. Hand it to him. "I'm going to miss having someone to talk to." You say. "But now you can write me. I can learn all about you. Like why they were so insistent in having you in here, pal. I had to fight Dr. Thanner everyday to get you out."

He looks at you and takes the paper. Just nods.You go home, feeling good about yourself. You brag to everyone you can tell, friends, family, classmates, co-workers, about how you came through for Arthur. You even fall asleep with a smile.That night, your eyes snap open. Screams, unearthly screams wake you up.

Then you see them. Your mother. Your father. Your friends. Your classmates. Your co-workers. Lying on your floor, their blood soaking into your carpet. Your walls stained with carnage. Their heads bashed in, their eyes missing from their sockets. Everyone you know dead or dying.

You whimper and see a man standing in the doorway.It's Arthur, holding the piece of paper you gave him.Your entire body shaking, you choke out. "Are you here to kill me?"

And Arthur just nods.

CHAPTER EIGHTEEN

Doors

I was adopted. I never knew my real mother; rather, I knew her at one time but I left her side when I was too little to be able to remember. I loved my adopted family though. They were so kind to me. I ate well, I lived in a warm and comfortable house, and I got to stay up pretty late.

Let me tell you about my family real fast: First, there's my mother. I never called her Mom or anything like that; I just called her by her first name. Janice. She didn't mind at all though. I called her that for so long, I don't think she even noticed. Anyhow, she was a very kind woman. I think that she is the one who recommended my adoption in the first place. Sometimes I would lay my head against her in front of the television and she would tickle my back with her nails. She is one of those Hollywood mothers.

Second, there's Dad. His real name was Richard, but he never really liked me much so I began to refer to him as Dad in a desperate attempt to gain his affection. It didn't work. I think that no matter what I called him, he would never love me as much as his own child. That's understandable so I really didn't press the matter. The most notable attribute of Dad was his unmoving sternness. He was not afraid to pop his children when they did something wrong. I found that out before I could use the restroom properly. He didn't hesitate to spank me. Well, I'm in line and it's because of his methods.

Lastly, is my sister. Little Emily was really young when I was adopted, so we were about the same age, but she was slightly older. I liked to think of her as my little sister, though. We got along better than any sibling could possibly get along.

We would always stay up late together and just talk. Well, she did a lot of the talking; I mostly just listened because I loved her. It was a great setup that we had! We were short on bedrooms, so- because I didn't want to sleep in the living room by myself when I was littler- I had a pallet set up for me next to her bed on the floor. This is where I have slept since. But it was cool with me because I enjoyed being with her and I had always felt pretty protective of my little sis.

Everything changed on a horrible Wednesday night. I was at home taking a nap when little Emily opened the front door. The sound of the door opening pulled me to a state of consciousness and I walked from the room down the hall to the living room. That's when I first remembered it was Wednesday. I was never any good at keeping track of what day it was. Actually I'll just go ahead and say it: My sense of time was HORRIBLE! But nevertheless, I knew it was Wednesday because Emily had just come home from her Church's youth group gathering. She walked in the front door and hugged me, and then was followed in by Dad and Janice.

"You have a good nap?" Janice said teasingly as she ruffled up my hair. I just shook my head away and snorted in a manner that clearly expressed that I was teasing back with her.

"Don't you snort at your mother like that!" said my father gruffly with authority. He shut the door behind him and hung up his coat.

"I was clearly joking..." I growled under my breath. He must not have heard me because I didn't feel him smack me. Emily then proceeded to our room and I followed. She started telling me about her day. You know... usual teenage girl stuff. But I listened so that she would feel better. After her summary she suggested watching TV and I obliged and jumped onto the couch as she was going for the remote.

She rolled her eyes at my little-brother-like immaturity and scooted me over and sat down. The TV turned on and we watched it together until the sun went down. Emily was the kind of girl that- instead of watching cartoons and soap operas- would rather watch Discovery and Animal Planet and Natural Geographic. I like those too so I didn't mind. Actually, those were the only channels that can hold my attention.

So it got late and Janice walked up behind the sofa. "Emily it's past your bed time. Turn off the television and go to your room. You too." she pointed at me. Emily turned off the program we were watching grudgingly and stood up. She started down the hallway to our room. As I followed I couldn't shake the feeling that something wasn't right.

We went into our room and Emily turned off the light. Just as she did, I caught a flash of movement out of the corner of my eye. It was out the window, but as soon as I redirected my line of sight to where the window was no longer in my peripheral vision, what it was that I thought I saw was gone. I still remained alert. For my sister's sake.

I laid there in the darkness with nothing but the thin ray of light from the street lamp outside to illuminate the room. It wasn't much. Time and time again I could have sworn that I heard subtle sounds just out the window... a twig break, leaves crunching, clothes jostling. And all the while I could smell a faint stench of sweat and blood. I kept my eyes open most of the night.

The sounds outside subsided and the smell left my nose. I began to feel at ease. My eyelids closed.

Not long after that, I heard a very loud crash on the other side of the house. I was up in an instant. "THERE'S SOMEONE IN THE HOUSE!" I barked with extreme adrenaline coursing through me. "Wake up!" I shrilly pleaded with Emily. She did, and as soon as I saw her sit up I ran to my parent's room...

Dad was dead. His neck was splayed open and gaping as blood spilled out of it, off the bed, and onto the floor. I saw that the master bathroom's door was closed and just before it- on the outside- was a man.A man... I don't feel comfortable calling it that.

He was very large and rugged. He turned around and saw me and that's when I saw him accurately for the first time. I wont forget it. His eyes were large and beady and trapped with lust. He was styling a beard that was badly unkempt with blood dripping off. His clothes were dirty and his face was cold. Just then I noticed the same horrid smell of sweat and blood from earlier, but this time it was overwhelming.

He saw me. He saw me and grinned with a set of crooked yellow teeth. That smile threw me off. I thought that I was going to die, but then he turned back to the bathroom door completely unperturbed by my presence. I was terrified and didn't no what to do. I just yelled and cried. I watched as he shouldered through door that was Mom's only protection. I watched as he raised the large razor that he was carrying, but had obviously neglected to use properly. I watched as he sliced her open and tore her to shreds...

I then heard something; the last thing that I wanted to hear... It was Emily's scream coming from behind me. The large monstrosity looked up from my butchered mother and stared at my little sister. I was distraught. He stood up and quickly started walking toward us. My sis turned and ran, and I was at a loss when he bypassed me and went straight after her. Why was she still in the house? Had she not assessed the situation and run? Apparently not, and now she was dead and I was alone.

I ran after them both. I expected the man to kill her as he had the rest of my family, but I was sadly mistaken. He grabbed her by the arm and jerked her as a way to make clear that he was in control. He dragged her through the house... I was making all of the noise I could now, hoping and praying that someone would come to my aid. He mustn't take her. Not her.

As he passed me I backed against the wall and whimpered with terror, "Why?" He didn't respond except by putting his free hand on my head while Emily screamed in the other and saying "Good boy." He gave another crooked grin and a very cold, unnatural laugh. I followed him to the door where he dragged my helpless sister after him. He opened it, pulled her out, and slammed it shut behind him.

I am now sitting in the house with my mutilated adopted parents, shivering and whimpering with dismay. He's out there with her. Doing who-knows-what to her, and I can't do anything. I would if I could, but I can't. I would chase after them in a heartbeat, but I can't. I sit here, looking at the front door. I look down at my paws. If only I could open doors...

CHAPTER NINETEEN

The Note

This is a love story. Please try to remember that as you read this, love. It's really about Julie.

I knew from the moment I set eyes on her that I'd do anything to have her. Fortunately though, I didn't have to work very hard. I could see it in her eyes the first time I talked to her and asked her out. She wanted me to and she said yes before I even finished asking. Her eyes sparkle like diamonds, it's one of my favorite things about her.

We were quick to say "I love you", only a few dates in, but we were sure.

My place is full of my idiot friends and we've started talking about getting a place of our own. My best friend, Greg, doesn't get along the best with her and isn't very happy about me moving out but he understands. We all hang out together sometimes, see movies, bowl, normal stuff like that.

Well, I got a call a couple nights ago from Julie's parents, who live out of state. They said they got a call from the police and that Julie had been in a car accident. Drunk driver crossed the center line, what a cliché right? Anyway, I was panicked out of my mind speeding like crazy to the hospital when Julie called me on my cell.

I could hardly believe my eyes when I saw her name on the called ID. I answered the phone not quite letting myself get my hopes up just yet. After all, it could have been someone calling me from her phone. Relief washed over me like rain when I heard her voice: "Baby? I'm okay, it wasn't that bad, just some bumps and bruises. The airbags and seat belt did all the work, are you okay?" I don't mind admitting, I pulled over and cried for a long time. She said she was checking out of the hospital shortly and I could pick her up there.

When I got to the hospital I had myself pretty well composed. I walked in and was just making my way to the help desk when I heard her call my name. I turned around and saw her, the sparkle was out of her eyes (which wasn't that surprising, I thought, considering what had happened), but otherwise seemingly none the worse for the wear. I completely lost what composure I thought I had. I broke down again and we held eachother and she slid her hand onto the back of my neck and into my hair like she does when I'm upset, and after a minute or two we made our way to my car.

Julie told me the drunk driver had been killed, and I thought "good, better him than Julie" and I'm not the least bit ashamed of it. I would have killed him myself if I could have. But she was OK and that was all I cared about then.

When we got back to my place no one was home and the house was dark, which was odd since there was almost always someone home and those idiot roommates of mine always forget to kill the lights when they leave.

Julie was feeling a little chilly and she looked a little pale so we cuddled up under some blankets and fell asleep almost immediately. It had been a trying day after all. I remember the last thing she said to me as we were falling asleep: "I'll love you forever, baby."

I called into work the next day to stay home with Julie, she was feeling pretty stiff, again not surprising. I had some missed calls from family and friends, no doubt they'd heard what happened and were checking in. I'd get back to them later.

Maybe it was just the accident, or that I hadn't seen Julie without makeup in... ever, but she didn't look very good, I mean her color was off and her eyes looked slightly hollow. And the sparkle still wasn't there. I suggested taking her back to the hospital, but she insisted she was fine, just tired and sore.

Well, a couple more days went by and I told work I was staying home with Julie until she was feeling better. But she wasn't getting better. Her eyes were the worst of it. More hollow all the time, and her skin was downright cold to the touch. It was getting to the point where I was going to bring her back to the hospital, whether she wanted to go or not, and that was when I got the phone call. It was Julie's mom. She had been crying and was clearly making an effort to stay composed.

Julie's service was to be held the day after tomorrow she said. I asked her what she was talking about, service for what? I was confused.

Julie walked up to me as I stood there on the phone. She was looking right into my eyes when her mom said "I know this is hard for you, it's hard for all of us, but Julie's gone and we can't bring her back, we all loved her but she's gone."

I still didn't understand until I saw the look of horror in Julie's eyes. She knew, this whole time she knew. She didn't survive the accident yet somehow she was here and suddenly I understood. Her eyes: hollow and sunk in, the sparkle gone. Her skin, cold and discolored. She was dead and I was watching her slowly decay! My stomach dropped and I felt myself fall. Julie caught me, and I felt her cold hands and felt the coldness for what it was, death. I heard her mom on the phone, a tiny voice calling my name over and over. I picked up the phone and told her I was listening, Julie silent the whole time. Her mom repeated that the service was the day after tomorrow and her body would be cremated at noon the next day. Numbly, I told her okay, thanked her, and told her I'd see her then.

I hung up the phone and Julie and I just stared at each other for a long time. There was no doubt now, I was looking at someone who was not alive. Eventually I said one word: How?

She said she didn't know, and she didn't care. And you know what? Neither did I.

She came with me to the service, and it wasn't like what happens in the movies, where people walk through her like she's not there or anything like that. They couldn't see her, that much was obvious, but somehow no one bumped into her, and when they made space for me, it seemed they made space for her to, although they didn't seem to know they were doing it.

When I talked to her parents she was with me, silent but strong, for me. When I viewed her body she was with me. Her hand, (cold now, so cold) finding that spot on my neck. She looked exactly as she always had, beautiful, healthy. But I knew it was makeup and artificial. Underneath she would look exactly like the Julie that had her cold hand on my neck. It was a hard thing, looking down at her, but she was so supportive and I knew this was why I loved her and couldn't be without her.

We left and went back to my place. My roommates were home but stayed out of our way as we went to my room. That night we didn't sleep, we just held each other and I didn't care at all how cold she was. We cried, and talked. Laughed at the funny memories and cried more. We didn't talk about what was happening or what was going to happen.

As darkness began to lose the battle and light filled the sky, a horrifying thought occurred to me, and somehow I knew it would be true. I was seeing Julie as she was. I mean, literally seeing her as her body was. And she was set to be cremated at noon. Do you understand? She was to be burned until nothing would be left but ash and I would have to watch it happen.

I was on the phone immediately to her parents, to the funeral home, to her church. No one would listen. They all thought it was grief. I felt rage and despair building inside me and was about to completely break down when I felt her hand on my neck, in that spot, and she turned my head so I was looking into her eyes, now very hollow and turning grotesque. She told me it was okay, it was okay. She told me she would love me forever and I knew in that moment what I was going to do.

Those last few hours we watched the sun come up and what became a beautiful day. We watched clouds turn into funny shapes. As noon approached I made an excuse to go to my closet and then we waited. When noon hit we were both crying again, but nothing happened. We were just starting to wonder what that meant when I saw the look in her eyes, just as before, she knew. She felt it before I saw it. She told me it didn't hurt, it doesn't hurt baby.

She began to smoke and her hair caught on fire. A cold calm set over me and I took her tight into my arms. The flames began to burn me to. She tried to push me away, to protect me. She fought my hold but her strength was fading. I could feel the flames now burning into me but I didn't care, I wouldn't let her go through this alone and I didn't need to live much longer anyway. We didn't scream, we just sat there together and burned. Her hair was gone and her face and skin turned black and I held her tighter and to my chest. I told her I'd love her forever and that I'd see her soon. I held her until she was ash in my arms and she fell through my fingers.

I reached for what I had taken out of the closet, and suddenly she was gone, not a trace of her left. No ash remained anywhere, nothing was burned, even my own burns were gone.Was it grief? Did I imagine the whole thing? Was she ever here? I don't know. But I wrote this so my family and friends know why I had to do this. I won't stay here without her. I can't. I'll find her somehow and the sparkle will be in her eyes again and everything will be okay and like it was. I'm sorry about this mom, dad. But I hope you understand. I'm going now, I hope I don't get blood on this

CHAPTER TWENTY

Jeff the Killer

Excerpt from a local Newspaper:

OMINOUS UNKNOWN KILLER IS STILL AT LARGE.

After weeks of unexplained murders, the ominous unknown killer is still on the rise. After little evidence has been found, a young boy states that he survived one of the killer's attacks and bravely tells his story.

"I had a bad dream and I woke up in the middle of the night," says the boy, "I saw that for some reason the window was open, even though I remember it being closed before I went to bed. I got up and shut it once more. Afterwards, I simply crawled under my covers and tried to get back to sleep. That's when I had a strange feeling, like someone was watching me.

I looked up, and nearly jumped out of my bed. There, in the little ray of light, illuminating from between my curtains, were a pair of two eyes. These weren't regular eyes; they were dark, ominous eyes. They were bordered in black and... just plain out terrified me. That's when I saw his mouth. A long, horrendous smile that made every hair on my body stand up. The figure stood there, watching me. Finally, after what seemed like forever, he said it. A simple phrase, but said in a way only a mad man could speak.

"He said, 'Go To Sleep.' I let out a scream, that's what sent him at me. He pulled up a knife; aiming at my heart. He jumped on top of my bed. I fought him back; I kicked, I punched, I rolled around, trying to knock him off me. That's when my dad busted in. The man threw the knife, it went into my dad's shoulder. The man probably would've finished him off, if one of the neighbors hadn't alerted the police.

"They drove into the parking lot, and ran towards the door. The man turned and ran down the hallway. I heard a smash, like glass breaking. As I came out of my room, I saw the window that was pointing towards the back of my house was broken. I looked out it to see him vanish into the distance. I can tell you one thing, I will never forget that face. Those cold, evil eyes, and that psychotic smile. They will never leave my head."

Police are still on the look for this man. If you see anyone that fits the description in this story, please contact your local police department.

Jeff and his family had just moved into a new neighborhood. His dad had gotten a promotion at work, and they thought it would be best to live in one of those "fancy" neighborhoods. Jeff and his brother Liu couldn't complain though. A new, better house. What was not to love? As they were getting unpacked, one of their neighbors came by.

"Hello," she said, "I'm Barbara; I live across the street from you. Well, I just wanted to introduce my self and to introduce my son." She turns around and calls her son over. "Billy, these are our new neighbors." Billy said hi and ran back to play in his yard.

"Well," said Jeff's mom, "I'm Margaret, and this is my husband Peter, and my two sons, Jeff and Liu." They each introduced themselves, and then Barbara invited them to her son's birthday. Jeff and his brother were about to object, when their mother said that they would love to. When Jeff and his family are done packing, Jeff went up to his mom.

"Mom, why would you invite us to some kid's party? If you haven't noticed, I'm not some dumb kid."

"Jeff," said his mother, "We just moved here; we should show that we want to spend time with our neighbors. Now, we're going to that party, and that's final." Jeff started to talk, but stopped himself, knowing that he couldn't do anything. Whenever his mom said something, it was final. He walked up to his room and plopped down on his bed. He sat there looking at his ceiling when suddenly, he got a weird feeling. Not so much a pain, but... a weird feeling. He dismissed it as just some random feeling. He heard his mother call him down to get his stuff, and he walked down to get it.

The next day, Jeff walked down stairs to get breakfast and got ready for school. As he sat there, eating his breakfast, he once again got that feeling. This time it was stronger. It gave him a slight tugging pain, but he once again dismissed it. As he and Liu finished breakfast, they walked down to the bus stop. They sat there waiting for the bus, and then, all of a sudden, some kid on a skateboard jumped over them, only inches above their laps. They both jumped back in surprise. "Hey, what the hell?"

The kid landed and turned back to them. He kicked his skate board up and caught it with his hands. The kid seems to be about twelve; one year younger than Jeff. He wears a Aeropostale shirt and ripped blue jeans.

"Well, well, well. It looks like we got some new meat." Suddenly, two other kids appeared. One was super skinny and the other was huge. "Well, since you're new here, I'd like to introduce ourselves, over there is Keith." Jeff and Liu looked over to the skinny kid. He had a dopey face that you would expect a sidekick to have. "And he's Troy." They looked over at the fat kid. Talk about a tub of lard. This kid looked like he hadn't exercised since he was crawling.

"And I," said the first kid, "am Randy. Now, for all the kids in this neighborhood there is a small price for bus fare, if you catch my drift." Liu stood up, ready to punch the lights out of the kid's eyes when one of his friends pulled a knife on him. "Tsk, tsk, tsk, I had hoped you would be more cooperative, but it seems we must do this the hard way." The kid walked up to Liu and took his wallet out of his pocket. Jeff got that feeling again. Now, it was truly strong; a burning sensation. He stood up, but Liu gestured him to sit down. Jeff ignored him and walked up to the kid.

"Listen here you little punk, give back my bro's wallet or else." Randy put the wallet in his pocket and pulled out his own knife.

"Oh? And what will you do?" Just as he finished the sentence, Jeff popped the kid in the nose. As Randy reached for his face, Jeff grabbed the kid's wrist and broke it. Randy screamed and Jeff grabbed the knife from his hand. Troy and Keith rushed Jeff, but Jeff was too quick. He threw Randy to the ground. Keith lashed out at him, but Jeff ducked and stabbed him in the arm. Keith dropped his knife and fell to the ground screaming. Troy rushd him too, but Jeff didn't even need the knife. He just punched Troy straight in the stomach and Troy went down. As he fell, he puked all over. Liu could do nothing but look in amazement at Jeff.

"Jeff how'd you?" that was all he said. They saw the bus coming and knew they'd be blamed for the whole thing. So they started running as fast as they could. As they ran, they looked back and saw the bus driver rushing over to Randy and the others. As Jeff and Liu made it to school, they didn't dare tell what happened. All they did was sit and listen. Liu just thought of that as his brother beating up a few kids, but Jeff knew it was more. It was something, scary.

As he got that feeling he felt how powerful it was, the urge to just, hurt someone. He didn't like how it sounded, but he couldn't help feeling happy. He felt that strange feeling go away, and stay away for the entire day of school. Even as he walked home due to the whole thing near the bus stop, and how now he probably wouldn't be taking the bus anymore, he felt happy. When he got home his parents asked him how his day was, and he said, in a somewhat ominous voice, "It was a wonderful day." Next morning, he heard a knock at his front door. He walked down to find two police officers at the door, his mother looking back at him with an angry look.

"Jeff, these officers tell me that you attacked three kids. That it wasn't regular fighting, and that they were stabbed. Stabbed, son!" Jeff's gaze fell to the floor, showing his mother that it was true.

"Mom, they were the ones who pulled the knives on me and Liu."

"Son," said one of the cops," We found three kids, two stabbed, one having a bruise on his stomach, and we have witnesses proving that you fled the scene. Now, what does that tell us?" Jeff knew it was no use. He could say him and Liu had been attacked, but then there was no proof it was not them who attacked first. They couldn't say that they weren't fleeing, because truth be told they were. So Jeff couldn't defend himself or Liu.

"Son, call down your brother." Jeff couldn't do it, since it was him who beat up all the kids.

"Sir, it…it was me. I was the one who beat up the kids. Liu tried to hold me back, but he couldn't stop me." The cop looked at his partner and they both nod.

"Well kid, looks like a year in Juvy…"

"Wait!" says Liu. They all looked up to see him holding a knife. The officers pulled their guns and locked them on Liu.

"It was me, I beat up those little punks. Have the marks to prove it." He lifted up his sleeves to reveal cuts and bruises, as if he was in a struggle.

"Son, just put the knife down," said the officer. Liu held up the knife and dropped it to the ground. He put his hands up and walked over to the cops.

"No Liu, it was me! I did it!" Jeff had tears running down his face.

"Huh, poor bro. Trying to take the blame for what I did. Well, take me away." The police led Liu out to the patrol car.

"Liu, tell them it was me! Tell them! I was the one who beat up those kids!" Jeff's mother put her hands on his shoulders.

"Jeff please, you don't have to lie. We know it's Liu, you can stop." Jeff watched helplessly as the cop car speeds off with Liu inside. A few minutes later Jeff's dad pulled into the driveway, seeing Jeff's face and knowing something was wrong.

"Son, son what is it?" Jeff couldn't answer. His vocal cords were strained from crying. Instead, Jeff's mother walked his father inside to break the bad news to him as Jeff wept in the driveway. After an hour or so Jeff walked back in to the house, seeing that his parents were both shocked, sad, and disappointed. He couldn't look at them. He couldn't see how they thought of Liu when it was his fault. He just went to sleep, trying to get the whole thing off his mind. Two days went by, with no word from Liu at JDC. No friends to hang out with. Nothing but sadness and guilt. That is until Saturday, when Jeff is woke up by his mother, with a happy, sunshiny face.

"Jeff, it's the day." she said as she opened up the curtains and let light flood into his room.

"What, what's today?" asked Jeff as he stirs awake.

"Why, it's Billy's party." He was now fully awake.

"Mom, you're joking, right? You don't expect me to go to some kid's party after..." There was a long pause.

"Jeff, we both know what happened. I think this party could be the thing that brightens up the past days. Now, get dressed." Jeff's mother walked out of the room and downstairs to get ready herself. He fought himself to get up. He picked out a random shirt and pair of jeans and walked down stairs. He saw his mother and father all dressed up; his mother in a dress and his father in a suit. He thought, why they would ever wear such fancy clothes to a kid's party?

"Son, is that all your going to wear?" said Jeff's mom.

"Better than wearing too much." he said. His mother pushed down the feeling to yell at him and hid it with a smile.

"Now Jeff, we may be over-dressed, but this is how you go if you want to make an impression." said his father. Jeff grunted and went back up to his room.

"I don't have any fancy clothes!" he yelled down stairs.

"Just pick out something." called his mother. He looked around in his closet for what he would call fancy. He found a pair of black dress pants he had for special occasions and an undershirt. He couldn't find a shirt to go with it though. He looked around, and found only striped and patterned shirts. None of which go with dress pants. Finally he found a white hoodie and put it on.

"You're wearing that?" they both said. His mother looked at her watch. "Oh, no time to change. Let's just go." She said as she herded Jeff and his father out the door. They crossed the street over to Barbara and Billy's house. They knocked on the door and at it appeared that Barbara, just like his parents, way over-dressed. As they walked inside all Jeff could see were adults, no kids.

"The kids are out in the yard. Jeff, how about you go and meet some of them?" said Barbara.

Jeff walked outside to a yard full of kids. They were running around in weird cowboy costumes and shooting each other with plastic guns. He might as well be standing in a Toys R Us. Suddenly a kid came up to him and handed him a toy gun and hat.

"Hey. Wanna pway?" he said.

"Ah, no kid. I'm way too old for this stuff." The kid looked at him with that weird puppydog face.

"Pwease?" said the kid. "Fine," said Jeff. He put on the hat and started to pretend shoot at the kids. At first he thought it was totally ridiculous, but then he started to actually have fun. It might not have been super cool, but it was the first time he had done something that took his mind off of Liu. So he played with the kids for a while, until he heard a noise. A weird rolling noise. Then it hit him. Randy, Troy, and Keith all jumped over the fence on their skateboards. Jeff dropped the fake gun and ripped off the hat. Randy looked at Jeff with a burning hatred.

"Hello, Jeff, is it?" he said. "We have some unfinished business." Jeff saw his bruised nose." I think we're even. I beat the crap out of you, and you get my brother sent to JDC."

Randy got an angry look in his eyes. "Oh no, I don't go for even, I go for winning. You may have kicked our asses that one day, but not today." As he said that Randy rushed at Jeff. They both fell to the ground. Randy punched Jeff in the nose, and Jeff grabbed him by the ears and head butted him. Jeff pushed Randy off of him and both rose to their feet. Kids were screaming and parents were running out of the house. Troy and Keith both pulled guns out of their pockets.

"No one interrupts or guts will fly!" they said. Randy pulled a knife on Jeff and stabbed it into his shoulder.

Jeff screamed and fell to his knees. Randy started kicking him in the face. After three kicks Jeff grabs his foot and twists it, causing Randy to fall to the ground. Jeff stood up and walked towards the back door. Troy grabbed him.

"Need some help?" He picks Jeff up by the back of the collar and throws him through the patio door. As Jeff tries to stand he is kicked down to the ground. Randy repeatedly starts kicking Jeff, until he starts to cough up blood.

"Come on Jeff, fight me!" He picks Jeff up and throws him into the kitchen. Randy sees a bottle of vodka on the counter and smashes the glass over Jeff's head.

"Fight!" He throws Jeff back into the living room.

"Come on Jeff, look at me!" Jeff glances up, his face riddled with blood. "I was the one who got your brother sent to JDC! And now you're just gonna sit here and let him rot in there for a whole year! You should be ashamed!" Jeff starts to get up.

"Oh, finally! you stand and fight!" Jeff is now to his feet, blood and vodka on his face. Once again he gets that strange feeling, the one in which he hasn't felt for a while. "Finally. He's up!" says Randy as he runs at Jeff. That's when it happens. Something inside Jeff snaps. His psyche is destroyed, all rational thinking is gone, all he can do, is kill. He grabs Randy and pile drives him to the ground. He gets on top of him and punches him straight in the heart. The punch causes Randy's heart to stop. As Randy gasps for breath. Jeff hammers down on him. Punch after punch, blood gushes from Randy's body, until he takes one final breath, and dies.

Everyone is looking at Jeff now. The parents, the crying kids, even Troy and Keith. Although they easily break from their gaze and point their guns at Jeff. Jeff see's the guns trained on him and runs for the stairs. As he runs Troy and Keith let out fire on him, each shot missing. Jeff runs up the stairs. He hears Troy and Keith follow up behind. As they let out their final rounds of bullets Jeff ducks into the bathroom. He grabs the towel rack and rips it off the wall. Troy and Keith race in, knives ready.

Troy swings his knife at Jeff, who backs away and bangs the towel rack into Troy's face. Troy goes down hard and now all that's left is Keith. He is more agile than Troy though, and ducks when Jeff swings the towel rack. He dropped the knife and grabbed Jeff by the neck. He pushed him into the wall. A thing of bleach fell down on top of him from the top shelf. It burnt both of them and they both started to scream. Jeff wiped his eyes as best as he could. He pulled back the towel rack and swung it straight into Keith's head. As he lay there, bleeding to death, he let out an ominous smile.

"What's so funny?" asked Jeff. Keith pulled out a lighter and switched it on. "What's funny," he said, "Is that you're covered in bleach and alcohol." Jeff's eyes widened as Keith threw the lighter at him. As soon as the flame made contact with him, the flames ignited the alcohol in the vodka.

While the alcohol burned him, the bleach bleached his skin. Jeff let out a terrible screech as he caught on fire. He tried to roll out the fire but it was no use, the alcohol had made him a walking inferno. He ran down the hall, and fell down the stairs. Everybody started screaming as they saw Jeff, now a man on fire, drop to the ground, nearly dead. The last thing Jeff saw was his mother and the other parents trying to extinguish the flame. That's when he passed out.

When Jeff woke he had a cast wrapped around his face. He couldn't see anything, but he felt a cast on his shoulder, and stitches all over his body. He tried to stand up, but he realized that there was some tube in his arm, and when he tried to get up it fell out, and a nurse rushed in."I don't think you can get out of bed just yet." she said as she put him back in his bed and re-inserted the tube. Jeff sat there, with no vision, no idea of what his surroundings were. Finally, after hours, he heard his mother.

"Honey, are you okay?" she asked. Jeff couldn't answer though, his face was covered, and he was unable to speak. "Oh honey, I have great news. After all the witnesses told the police that Randy confessed of trying to attack you, they decided to let Liu go." This made Jeff almost bolt up, stopping halfway, remembering the tube coming out of his arm. "He'll be out by tomorrow, and then you two will be able to be together again."

Jeff's mother hugs Jeff and says her goodbyes. The next couple of weeks were those where Jeff was visited by his family. Then came the day where his bandages were to be removed. His family were all there to see it, what he would look like. As the doctors unwrapped the bandages from Jeff's face everyone was on the edge of their seats. They waited until the last bandage holding the cover over his face was almost removed.

"Let's hope for the best," said the doctor. He quickly pulls the cloth; letting the rest fall from Jeff's face.

Jeff's mother screams at the sight of his face. Liu and Jeff's dad stare awe-struck at his face.

"What? What happened to my face?" Jeff said. He rushed out of bed and ran to the bathroom. He looked in the mirror and saw the cause of the distress. His face. It...it's horrible. His lips were burnt to a deep shade of red. His face was turned into a pure white color, and his hair singed from brown to black. He slowly put his hand to his face. It had a sort of leathery feel to it now. He looked back at his family then back at the mirror.

"Jeff," said Liu, "It's not that bad...."

"Not that bad?" said Jeff," It's perfect!" His family were equally surprised. Jeff started laughing uncontrollably His parents noticed that his left eye and hand were twitching.

"Uh... Jeff, are you okay?"

"Okay? I've never felt more happy! Ha ha ha ha ha haaaaaa, look at me. This face goes perfectly with me!" He couldn't stop laughing. He stroked his face feeling it. Looking at it in the mirror. What caused this? Well, you may recall that when Jeff was fighting Randy something in his mind, his sanity, snapped. Now he was left as a crazy killing machine, that is, his parents didn't know.

"Doctor," said Jeff's mom, "Is my son... alright, you know. In the head?"

"Oh yes, this behavior is typical for patients that have taken very large amounts of pain killers. If his behavior doesn't change in a few weeks, bring him back here, and we'll give him a psychological test."

"Oh thank you doctor." Jeff's mother went over to Jeff." Jeff, sweety. It's time to go."

Jeff looks away from the mirror, his face still formed into a crazy smile. "Kay mommy, ha ha haaaaaaaaaaaa!" his mother took him by the shoulder and took him to get his clothes.

"This is what came in," said the lady at the desk. Jeff's mom looked down to see the black dress pants and white hoodie her son wore. Now they were clean of blood and now stitched together. Jeff's mother led him to his room and made him put his clothes on. Then they left, not knowing that this was their final day of life.

Later that night, Jeff's mother woke to a sound coming from the bathroom. It sounded as if someone was crying. She slowly walked over to see what it was. When she looked into the bathroom she saw a horrendous sight. Jeff had taken a knife and carved a smile into his cheeks.

"Jeff, what are you doing?" asked his mother.

Jeff looked over to his mother. "I couldn't keep smiling mommy. It hurt after awhile. Now, I can smile forever. Jeff's mother noticed his eyes, ringed in black.

"Jeff, your eyes!" His eyes were seemingly never closing.

"I couldn't see my face. I got tired and my eyes started to close. I burned out the eyelids so I could forever see myself; my new face." Jeff's mother slowly started to back away, seeing that her son was going insane. "What's wrong mommy? Aren't I beautiful?

"Yes son," she said, "Yes you are. L-let me go get daddy, so he can see your face." She ran into the room and shook Jeff's dad from his sleep. "Honey, get the gun we....." She stopped as she saw Jeff in the doorway, holding a knife.

"Mommy, you lied." That's the last thing they hear as Jeff rushes them with the knife, gutting both of them.

His brother Liu woke up, startled by some noise. He didn't hear anything else, so he just shut his eyes and tried to go back to sleep. As he was on the border of slumber, he got the strangest feeling that someone was watching him. He looked up, before Jeff's hand covered his mouth. He slowly raised the knife ready to plunge it into Liu. Liu thrashed here and there trying to escape Jeff's grip.

"Shhhhhhh," Jeff said,"Just go to sleep."

www.ingramcontent.com/pod-product-compliance
Lightning Source LLC
Chambersburg PA
CBHW031415160726
47993CB00003B/1242